More Than You Know

생각보다 훨씬 좋아해!

WRITTEN BY YEMARO

EDITIO
PUBLISHING

More Than You Know

© YEMARO

Cover Illustration by DOVE

생각보다 훨씬 좋아해! by 예마로

Copyright © 2021 by 예마로

All rights reserved.

This English edition was published by Editio Publishing LLC in 2023 by exclusive contract with KIDARISTUDIO, Inc.

ISBN 978-1-959742-20-3 (Print)

Printed in the United States of America

https://editiopublishing.com/

More Than You Know

CONTENTS

CHAPTER
THIRTY-ONE

After Arwen quietly left the room, Kendrick sat there for a while, staring blankly at the table. The floor was littered with broken china, and the leftover refreshments still sat on the table. He needed to summon the servants with the bell pull, but his mind wasn't working.

After a while, one of the maids who had been alerted by Arwen about the mess nervously knocked on the door.

"Your Grace, I was told..." The maid cautiously entered the room and let out a surprised yell as she caught sight of the broken teacup. "Oh! Your Grace! Your favorite teacup!"

"Hmm? Oh... I see," Kendrick answered in a daze.

It was a valuable tea set that Kendrick himself rarely used, but cheerfully insisted on using whenever Arwen visited. However, now, he seemed to barely even register that the precious cup was broken. He had too much to think about.

On their way to the Academy, Arwen's sudden declaration of independent living arrangements had left Kendrick reeling. Had that really been Arwen? Had his eyesight become so bad that he was confusing Arwen and Rietta?

Though this train of thought seemed ridiculous, Kendrick was convinced that it was a reasonable doubt. Arwen had always been a gentle child who had never gotten into trouble. They had even been worried that she was maybe too docile, so where was this coming from? She was barely twenty-two and not nearly old enough to move out.

...Over my dead body!

If Kendrick possessed any less self-control, he might have blurted out those words. But Kendrick was wise, having raised three children, and had managed to calmly tell her they would discuss it later.

But the more he thought about it, the more agitated he became. He had no way of keeping Arwen here. Legally, she was an adult, and she was not related to him or Marias in any way.

When Arwen had first asked them to sponsor her, they'd agreed wholeheartedly. It was the best they could do at the time. Arwen had felt uncomfortable with Kendrick and Marias, and creating a parent-child relationship was no easy task. They had been content to wait until Arwen was ready to accept them. But as the days turned into years, Arwen continued to keep her distance. It was evident in the way she refused to drop their titles when addressing them, and in the way she refused to lean on anyone and insisted on resolving issues on her own. Kendrick and Marias were only human, so they did feel a bit hurt, but they'd still thought it best to give the child more time.

But, sweetie, you want to move out? You just turned twenty-two!

In Kendrick's eyes, Arwen was still the skinny little girl he had met years ago. A child like that, living alone on the unsafe outskirts of the capital? He had no intention of allowing it so long as he lived.

The good news was that he knew Shuell was going to propose to Arwen that day.

Kendrick thought Shuell wasn't a bad match for Arwen. Arranged marriages were common among the nobility, anyway. Objectively speaking, Shuell was a great catch. He had an excellent family background and was good-natured. He had no criminal records, such as for drug use, tax evasion, or violence.

Above all, he loved Arwen, so he would be loyal to her and take good care of her. And even if that wasn't the case, Kendrick and Marias could still keep her close and protect her. She'd be getting a cute sister-in-law... and her parents-in-law wouldn't be bad, either.

But Arwen said she'd reject his proposal. Deprived of his

last resort, Kendrick was lost in thought.

Is there someone she likes? But all her friends are girls... Maybe she likes a girl. Same-sex marriage isn't legal in this kingdom, though. Oh no... wait, that's not the issue right now.

Kendrick, who was starting to think about ways to legalize same-sex marriage by getting back into politics, finally got a hold of himself.

His main concern was that he had run out of excuses to keep Arwen here. And that he had dumped this very important matter onto his wife. Kendrick knew better than anyone that Marias was a poor talker. Arwen, on the other hand, could convince anyone that the sky was green, so there was no way Marias would be able to persuade her.

The problems didn't stop there.

Despite Kendrick's best efforts over the years, Marias had always been soft on those she loved. How that conversation would end was obvious. Arwen's quiet, but persuasive, manner would win over Marias, who would immediately say "Sure" and allow Arwen to do as she wished.

Kendrick was running out of time. He would not have the opportunity to coach Marie. He just had to prevent Arwen from meeting her.

"Rita! I need a quill and some paper. And a messenger to send to Marie. Quickly!"

I thought I would have to wait until the evening to see Marias, who'd gone to the palace, but I was able to meet her sooner than I thought. As I left Kendrick's reception room to head to my own room, a carriage entered the front gates.

Heading downstairs, I saw Marias handing her cloak to the butler. She had her black hair up in a ponytail and was wearing the uniform of the royal knights. It was a sight that would have had Rietta clenching her jaw in envy as well as respect. That's how great Marias looked in her uniform.

All right. Let's not be sour about whatever she is going to say. Kendrick himself isn't protesting.

Marias had simply not handed over her authority to her husband. She was still her own person.

I took a deep breath and smiled brightly. "Welcome home, Marie."

Marias looked up at the sound of my voice. "Oh, Wen." Her face was as expressionless as always, but her eyes had softened. It meant that she was in a particularly good mood.

Before I could say anything else, she pulled out a box from her uniform pocket and held it out to me.

"What's this?"

Marias' eyes sparkled. "Open it."

What had her so excited? I opened the box. Inside it was a small key, a silver one with a flower bud-shaped ruby on the head of it.

What is this?

"It's the key to the Severilous treasure vault."

"Excuse me?"

"The vault is in—"

"N-no, no, wait!" I hurriedly interrupted.

It wasn't appropriate for me to hear about this in the foyer with other people around, and I was baffled by the idea of receiving the key to their family treasure vault. The key was usually kept by the lady of the house. Occasionally, if the lady of the house had a good relationship with her daughter-in-law, she would give her a copy of the key, but this rarely happened as it meant handing over her authority.

"Don't tell Derick. He is preparing as well," said Marias, who had been eyeing me, when I didn't reply.

Those words were even more confusing. Was Derick waiting to have this key?

"Then why—"

Why are you giving this to me, then? I was about to ask— when a servant came running up to us.

"Y-Your Grace!"

Before he could even catch his breath, the servant looked at me, then at Marie, and the color drained from his flushed face. Without so much as offering a proper greeting, he handed what he was carrying to Marias. It was a letter that hadn't even been sealed.

Seeing the urgency in the servant's eyes, Marias quickly read the letter. Her face grew somber as her eyes flew over the words.

"Good heavens."

My heart sank at the words she said while folding the parchment. Marias rarely lost her composure. What had happened to make her say that?

"Marie, what is it?"

As soon as I spoke, her demeanor changed. It was as if the genre had changed from an action movie to an arcade puzzle game.

In other words, Marias was behaving awkwardly.

"Umm... you... see..."

I tilted my head in confusion, but before I could ask what was wrong, Marie stiffly turned away from me.

"I have an urgent matter to tend to. I must go."

"Oh... all right. Goodbye."

That was a bit weird, but the way she froze while reading the letter wasn't an act.

When I didn't object, Marias hurriedly walked away. At the foot of the stairs, she turned her head toward me. I could see her face, which was unsettlingly rigid and in turmoil.

"Take good care of that key," Marie said robotically, and quickly turned away again to climb the stairs. Instead of the third floor, where her office was located, she headed to the second floor. Derick's reception room was on that floor.

I watched her retreating figure with a puzzled expression. Did she have some matter to discuss with Derick?

CHAPTER
THIRTY-TWO

A few days later, I was pondering.

I shouldn't have let Marias go.

I reminded myself that the Severilouses were a family of warriors. Marias tended to let us win arguments, as if she had no experience of conflict, but there was no way she hadn't rightfully earned her position as the captain of the Royal Knight Order. Kendrick was a born civil servant, but he had learned some fighting skills when he married into this family. I had lived with them for a long time, but the Severilous family members really were different.

There hadn't been a chance to bring up the proposal with Derick and Marie. There was no sign of them at all. We were living in the same house, yet I hadn't come across even a shadow. They were so good at hiding that an ordinary person had no way of finding them.

How am I supposed to talk to them if I can't even catch a glimpse of them?

I had been drinking tea to calm myself, but ended up putting down my teacup so forcefully that it clattered loudly.

This was getting ridiculous.

My resolve to have a serious talk with Marie and Derick faded when they didn't show up to dinner for the third day in a row. They never missed dinner, even when they were busy. It was clear that they were avoiding me.

In the end, I gave up. If they wanted to avoid talking to me that badly, I had no choice. Instead, I decided to push the task onto someone who was much easier to deal with.

Two o'clock at the orangery. Before the tea I had poured could cool down even a fraction, a mop of blond hair popped up in the distance.

I didn't get up. I sat there, waiting, as Shuell approached cautiously.

"Umm, Wen..."

"Sit down."

At my command, Shuell immediately sat down across from me.

He had a tense expression on his face, and his lips were pressed together tightly, so I told him the words I had thought over at least a hundred times.

"I've said it before, but I'm turning down your proposal. I'm sorry about the rumor the servants seem to believe, but I hope you will correct them. And tell Marie and Derick that."

Shuell nodded obediently. At the sight of his glum

expression, I sighed and poured him some tea. Whatever his intentions were, it was true that things had gotten complicated for me because of Shuell's proposal, so he had been feeling guilty these past few days. I wavered between feeling sorry for him and feeling annoyed by him—but seeing him so crestfallen didn't sit well with me.

"Why don't you want to marry me, Wen?"

I froze mid-pour. I met his eyes with an exasperated expression on my face. "What?"

"I've got a good background, a nice personality, and good looks... probably." He listed each one off on his fingers, then tilted his head to the side. "I'm quite the catch, aren't I?"

Never mind. I'm not sorry for him.

"You really are self-assured, aren't you?" I felt a bit dumbstruck. What was I supposed to do with his ego? Sure, his looks and background were good, so his statement wasn't entirely baseless. But it was so obnoxious.

"I'm just saying that I'm good husband material. Don't you intend to get married someday, Wen?"

My expression must have been very solemn because Shuell hurriedly waved his hands in denial.

Only then did I concede. I understood what he was saying. Most nobles got married, and they did so at an early age, so as to have children and continue the family line. It was rare, but some even married after getting pregnant, and one of the most important reasons for making your debut in high society was to find yourself a suitor.

Marriage was a necessity in this society.

Shuell and I were both at the perfect age to get married. I could also guarantee that he was the best of the eligible bachelors that I—or any lady at a marriageable age—could choose.

But just because it was true didn't mean that I was happy to acknowledge it.

Seriously, he'd be much less annoying if he wasn't so self-aware.

Instead of answering him, I let out a huff of laughter, stepped over to Shuell, and smacked his back—*hard*.

"Gah!" Shuell doubled over and looked as though he might start to cry. It did sound like it had hurt.

I patted his wide shoulders as he hunched in pain and, smiling, quietly told him, "If I wanted to use you to make a profit, I would have asked for a reward for returning you to your parents when we were nine instead of marrying you now."

I was completely exasperated at how shameless he must have thought I was. Sure, if I did marry him, I would have a lot to gain. But what about Shuell?

A fair transaction was only possible when both parties had something to gain. If anything, Shuell would lose out by marrying me.

"You can't make me let you go through such a disadvantageous marriage, Shuell."

His expression had grown solemn. Realizing that I must have triggered his childhood trauma, I quickly changed the subject.

"I don't want to get married out of necessity. I would like to live alone, and if I do ever meet someone I want to marry..." I wanted to keep ranting, but I seemed to have chosen the wrong subject. I stayed quiet for a moment.

Hmm. I'm not actually sure I'll ever find someone suitable.

But now wasn't the time for me to agonize over this. I shrugged.

"In any case, I'm going to pack my things and leave as soon as possible. Tell Marie and Derick that if they refuse to talk to me, I'll be notifying them through a letter."

It felt wrong even as I said it. But what else was I supposed to do when they refused to even see me?

Shuell still looked troubled as he stared at me. But before he could say anything, we heard a familiar voice.

"Wen."

I stilled for a moment. When I turned around, Marie

and Derick were standing there. It didn't look as though I could just welcome them as if nothing had happened. Their expressions were rigid, as if they had been slapped in the face.

A heavy, almost eerie silence fell until Derick, his face pale, managed to open his mouth.

"Let us talk for a moment."

Derick's reception room was unbelievably frigid. No one dared to speak first.

I sat there, in the uneasy, cold atmosphere, unable to even look around. I had planned to pretend to be mad for a little while and then accept their apology once Marie and Derick showed their faces again. I had thought that even if things might get serious while talking about important matters, that wouldn't last long, and things would go back to normal right away. I never imagined Derick and Marie would look so intimidating and conflicted.

Unaware of what was going on inside their heads, I watched them warily. I hadn't even noticed them entering the orangery because I had been busy talking to Shuell. Were they acting this way because they overheard what I said? But I didn't say anything particularly problematic...

"First of all, let me apologize for avoiding you these past few days." Derick was the first to speak up. "It was because we did not know what to tell you. Be that as it may, avoiding you was not very mature of us. We are sorry, Wen."

"No, it's all right," I mumbled. It wasn't like I could reject such a sincere apology.

Derick let out an exhale that felt colder to me than the winter wind. "We went to see you when we heard you were at the orangery with Shuell, but we accidentally overheard you talking."

I nodded.

Derick's voice, which had sounded calm so far, trembled when he continued. "Why..." He looked as if he were about to either cry or fly off the handle. "Why did you say you were not a good match for Shuell?"

I found myself at a loss for words. It felt as though the thoughts that had slipped out of my mouth were now back-stabbing me.

"I..." I smiled uncomfortably. It wasn't something I wanted to talk about. "There's no specific reason."

Derick pressed his lips together firmly. "My dear, could it be..." After a long moment, he finally said something completely unexpected. "That you dislike us?"

My eyes widened.

"Did you stay because you had nowhere else to go, but deep down..." Derick bit down on his lower lip. He sounded as though he was in pain as he finished his question. "Did you dislike staying with us?"

"No!" I exclaimed without hesitating. This, at least, I was sure about. "No, not at all. Really. Of course not!"

Everything that had happened at the duke's estate had been unbelievably wonderful. How could I ever dislike any of that?

At my immediate reply, Derick and Marie brightened up a little.

"Was there anything that made you uncomfortable?" Derick asked.

I wasn't sure what he meant by that, but I shook my head.

"When we overheard you, we were shocked," Derick said softly, looking a bit less agitated than before. "We were worried we had made you feel mistreated in some way. So, we thought that you wanted to leave since you disliked us because of something we did."

As I listened to his kind words, I shook my head. Derick was usually very perceptive, but for once he was wrong. The reason I said that was much more down-to-earth and self-deprecating.

"Why are you saying you want to leave, Wen? And so hurriedly at that?" Derick asked quietly.

But that was a question that had a lot to do with the subject I was trying to avoid.

I kept my mouth shut because I couldn't think of a good answer right away. Everyone at the Severilous estate was kind to me, and I loved them. But this wasn't about that. More specifically, it was about something that couldn't be changed, as much as I loved everyone.

"I just..."

I didn't want to talk about it. But I didn't want Derick to think I didn't like them, either.

"I..." I chewed on my lip until I managed to blurt out, "I'm just a temporary guest."

It felt as though the words I had finally spoken were lodged in my throat. I took a deep breath. My mind was like an overflowing storage room crowded with thoughts. The Severilous mansion was beautiful, peaceful, and lovely, but I wasn't always happy here.

Because I felt like I didn't really belong.

Marie and Derick, the duke and duchess, were always kind to me, and thanks to them, my childhood was full of wonderful memories. It wasn't that I wasn't thankful for that. But at the same time, I knew.

I knew that taking me in was only a show of goodwill that didn't require much effort, similar to how I had saved Shuell simply because I felt guilty. I was a young girl who wouldn't cause any trouble whether they kept me or turned me away. His parents were good people, so of course, they had chosen to take me in.

No, it wasn't even because they were good people. Anyone would have made that choice—people don't want to become villains without gaining something from it. For them, raising one more child did not affect their finances at all, and it wasn't as though I was particularly annoying or got into a lot of trouble.

Shuell and Rietta were their children. Shuell, who had only been scolded halfheartedly even though he had gotten himself kidnapped and cost them an unimaginable amount of money, and Rietta, whom they had adopted even when everyone had criticized them for taking in a commoner. Shuell was right. He was from an affluent and noble family, and he had a gentle personality and beautiful looks.

But it was because he was so perfect that I could never be with him.

I didn't have any of those things, so of course I wasn't good enough for him. That was why I wanted to leave. The family was kind to me, and I loved them for it, but the mansion had never been my home.

It wasn't as though I had never seen a case where an adoption ended happily. Rietta had totally merged into the family, even though they weren't biologically related. But I knew from experience that such a thing didn't apply to my life.

I forced my lips, which threatened to droop at the corners, into a smile. I knew it wouldn't look convincing, but it was better than frowning.

"I'm just someone who will stay here for a short while."

CHAPTER
THIRTY-THREE

It really was one of those countless inevitable things in life. I'd been aware of that from a very young age.

"If I married Shuell, or even if I just got engaged to him, it would be a scandal. You might be able to keep it under control for now, but what about later?" To me, Marie and Derick's confident attitudes bordered on baseless bravado. "All kinds of problems will arise if a commoner like me becomes a lady of the Severilous family, and then..." I paused for a moment, unable to continue. I took a deep breath. "I'm sure you would want us to break off our engagement as soon as possible."

I'd intended to stay calm as I talked, but a touch of resentment made it into that last part. I bit my lip, hating myself for it. I didn't think that I didn't matter to them at all. But even if they treated me like their own child, at the end of the day, blood was thicker than water. To them, I was the least valuable of all. Compared to Shuell, Rietta, and the Severilous name they would inherit, I was unimportant enough to be abandoned at any time.

"Wen—"

"I'm sorry if I was out of line. I'm not trying to blame you." My hurried apology cut off Derick's reply.

I wanted to act like nothing was wrong, but I knew it wasn't working. The feelings I had repressed for so long were bubbling up. It wasn't their fault. Even if everything I'd just described were to happen and they demanded the engagement be broken, the duke and duchess would only be taking back the kindness they had shown me so far. It didn't matter whether or not it was harsh. I had no right to complain.

Still, even if they didn't agree, Marie and Derick were like parents to me. I didn't want to be pushed into a situation that would test the depth of their love for me. Expecting it was one thing; experiencing it would be another. Being abandoned by my parents for the third time would be too much.

My vision blurred, and a single tear fell from my eye. I quickly wiped it away. I could see Derick and Marie looking at me.

"You..." Marie said.

They looked confused and shocked.

"Don't tell me you've been thinking that all this time," Derick said.

And angry.

My heart dropped to the pit of my stomach.

"Wen, we are adults and more mature than you. But that doesn't mean we don't get hurt." Derick rubbed his face with his hands. Marie watched me with an intense look in her eyes. "We... are going to need to have a long conversation about this."

They had never before acted like this toward me. They had always been gentle, even when they had disciplined me, and they certainly had never been angry with me. My fingertips grew cold, and my hands began to tremble. I felt wronged, but also scared.

At that very moment, I was not twenty-two. I was the little nine-year-old girl trembling in front of my parents' room, scared that they would hate me.

"We have spent over ten years together now." It was Marie, who had kept quiet until now, who broke the silence in the reception room.

I could have guessed what would follow, but my mind was blank from exhaustion. I chewed my lip, feeling that whatever it was, it probably wasn't good.

"You are our child. Just like Shuell and Rietta."

When I heard those words, I felt numb. I forgot about the fact that my hands were trembling.

I never expected this.

Marie smiled weakly. She had always seemed so strong,

and I had never seen her smile like that. She walked toward me and wrapped me in a tight embrace. It was still as warm as ever. Derick seemed a bit angrier, but he wrapped his arms around me as well, then he and Marie left the room. Left alone, I sat there, dazed.

Their words and their warmth lingered.

Kendrick sped up as soon as they left the room. Marias quietly followed him, and it was only when they had walked up the stairs, reached their room at the end of the hallway, and closed the door behind them, that he spoke, shaking.

"Arwen is just so... That child!" He was a mess of sorrow and anger as he pressed his lips together tightly. "A temporary guest? How could she? How could she say that to me?"

Marias looked troubled as she watched him exclaim through gritted teeth. When she led her agitated husband to the couch and held his hand, he used the other to rub his face.

"That girl is my daughter. Our daughter. You know that, Marie." His sorrowful eyes searched for understanding as they turned to his wife.

Arwen, who had already acted like an adult at age nine, was their dear child. They weren't related by blood, but because of that, they had made sure to pay more attention to her. Just like Shuell and Rietta, Arwen was everything to them.

"I raised that girl as my daughter for thirteen years, but all that time she had been thinking of us as strangers."

It felt like a slap in the face when they had heard Arwen say as much with a forced smile. Hearing your beloved daughter call you a stranger was painful. But they couldn't blame her for it.

"It's so upsetting, and cold-hearted, and mean, but..." Kendrick's voice sank as if he was about to cry. "Marie, did you see her face?"

Marias nodded. "She looked like she was about to cry but couldn't shed a single tear."

The painful memory of that exact expression was what had rendered them unable to get angry at her and instead made them leave the room and move out of earshot.

"It was just like that day, thirteen years ago."

She had barely reached their waists back then. They could still clearly remember the face of that tiny girl, pale as a ghost and staring up at them. They should have sent her back, but that face had haunted them, and they couldn't bear to do that to her.

And that little girl had grown on them.

At first, they had simply pitied her and opened themselves up only a little, but then Arwen had completely taken over all of their hearts. They had known that she was emotionally scarred and had done their best to welcome her, and Arwen had taken to them quickly. She had opened her heart in return, and the shadow over her had cleared.

"I thought... I thought she had gotten better," Kendrick said. That was what they had thought until today, until they had talked to Arwen. "I was complacent, like a fool. I thought she was fine, just because we loved her." He sighed deeply—an exhale full of complex feelings.

Marias looked anguished. "We should have known, Derick," she said softly. "We knew exactly why she had gotten so mature. The whole time we were at ease, Arwen never stopped being that lonely child." Marias' quiet words were reproachful. Toward her husband and herself.

"Do you think it's too late?" Kendrick's words turned into sobs. "I-I don't know what to do. What do we do now?"

His eyes swam with tears as he wondered how they could comfort her. They'd found out far too late. Arwen must have spent all those years thinking that she wasn't truly a part of the family. What if, like when she declared that she would leave with a carefree smile, she had already isolated herself? What if her wounds were already too deep to heal?

"What can we do, Marie?"

Marias, who had been watching her teary husband with a sorrowful gaze, slowly wrapped her arms around him.

"It'll be all right."

Derick didn't say anything in return.

"Wen will get better. I know it," she muttered as if assuring herself. She was just as lost as he was. But Marias had hope. "Let's tell her we love her more often. Just like you did for me, for Shuell, and for Rietta."

She and Kendrick loved Arwen, and Marias knew just how vast and delicate her husband's love was.

"It may be difficult, but we can do it. Like you said, we are her parents." Marias had no doubt that their genuine love would point them in the right direction.

"Do you think that will be enough?"

Kendrick still seemed anxious. Marias held her husband tighter and chuckled. "It will be."

Even if we're not enough, even if we make mistakes.

We aren't the only ones who love her, after all.

After Marie and Derick had left, I sat in the empty reception room like an abandoned doll, contemplating what they told me.

"Wen, we are adults and more mature than you, but that doesn't mean we don't get hurt."

"You are our child. Just like Shuell and Rietta."

Come to think of it, we had spent an exceptionally long time together, and during that whole time, they never stopped being kind to me. It wasn't as though they had anything to gain by earning my affection. That had to mean that their words were sincere.

"This is good," I forced myself to mumble.

That's right, I was lonely. I wished I had my own family, my own parents.

Though I called Marie and Derick by name, they had been like my parents this whole time. So, all I had to do now was be happy that I had become their daughter. That was all...

In a daze, I hung my head. The pale face of a woman stared back at me, reflected in my tea. Unable to meet her eyes, I buried my face in my hands.

I just couldn't believe it. Their words had been kind, and I was thankful for them. But that didn't mean that I could believe what they had said.

I knew some parents loved their adopted children as they would their own. I knew this very well—since Marie and Derick had raised Rietta with that kind of love. I knew that. I really did. But there was a memory etched deeply into my brain that I simply couldn't forget.

A memory from my past life in the other world.

I was eleven years old when I was sent to an orphanage in my past life.

I was old enough to know what was going on. But at the time, I wasn't sad to be sent to an orphanage. In my past life, my parents had not been good people, to put it mildly. Domestic abusers—a term often heard on the news—that was what they were. Thanks to a kind neighbor reporting them numerous times, and after a rigorous process, I was finally able to escape from them.

There were many kids like me at the orphanage, and it wasn't a particularly peaceful place, but I was fairly content to be there. Violence occurred between the children, but it was much milder than the abuse I had suffered from adults, and most of the kids there were younger than I was. The adults tended to ignore me since they were so busy and I was older, but I was happy that they didn't hit me or curse at me. Most importantly, it was where I made my first friend. Unlike me, boisterous and rough, she was quiet and shy. Since we were around the same age, we grew close pretty quickly and would always be together.

When a year had gone by and I had gotten used to the orphanage, I met someone.

"Hello. Are you ███████?"

The orphanage was always short-staffed, so volunteers came and went. But that was the first time an adult had called my name in such a kind manner. She was a lot like my friend, who always spoke quietly.

"Yes, why?"

She smiled at my slightly curt reply. "I see. It's nice to meet you," she said, extending a hand toward me. "I've been wanting to meet you. Would you like to be friends?"

A playful offer. Twelve-year-old me took her hand, puzzled. She told me to call her "Ma'am," and I wordlessly nodded.

That night, lying in bed, I took my friend's hand and muttered, "Do you think she'll be back?" Volunteers came and went whenever they pleased. Some would come by for months on end, while others never returned.

I hope she comes back.

My friend tightened her grip on my hand. "I hope she doesn't."

"Why? Was she a bad person?"

"Never mind." She turned away from me, uncharacteristically cold. I was confused but didn't try to comfort her.

Despite her wishes and my worries, the woman soon came by the orphanage again. And after that, she continued to visit. Whenever she came by, she spent a lot of time with us, and she changed our world.

I was a child who didn't know right from wrong and simply mimicked other people's behavior, and this was the first time someone had been so kind to me. My entire attitude, my manners, my beliefs—they all came from her. She taught me how to express my feelings without being violent, how to empathize with others, and how to love myself.

I learned how to love from her.

She taught me everything a parent should teach their child, and she taught me how to be affectionate. She was a good person, and she invested a lot of time in teaching me without getting angry at me. She adored me.

A lot of time passed before I got used to it all, and by

then, my friend had opened her heart to her as well. We'd grown close, and the woman started visiting the orphanage more often. The director didn't want the volunteers to get too attached to the children, but she never stopped this woman from spending time with us. I began to nurture a small flame of hope.

Maybe she was going to adopt me.

Sometimes, an overactive imagination hides the truth. That was why I didn't understand why she shook her head whenever I asked if I could call her "Mother."

She volunteered at the orphanage for exactly one year. On the last day, she adopted my friend, who had been with me all the time.

That day, my friend cried in her embrace. The woman cried as well. I watched them from afar.

There had been a reason my friend had disliked her and yet cried all night, saying whenever she visited that she missed her mother. A reason the woman had been so eager to do everything for my friend even when my friend pushed her away.

It was only when I overheard the director saying that she must be glad that her biological daughter had finally opened her heart that I understood everything.

Their faces were bright when they left the orphanage.

Everyone said that they were happy for them, except for me. They both tried to comfort me when I cried. She took me in her arms and patted my back as she told me, "████████, I'll come see you often. I'll bring Yeonsoo along and visit you often, okay? Don't cry. How am I supposed to say goodbye with a smile if you keep crying?"

She was so kind. As she consoled me, her voice was full of pity. That was why I couldn't possibly ask her to take me with her too.

Unsurprisingly, her visits to the orphanage became rarer. I threw tantrums and yelled at her to visit more often, but she looked conflicted as she tried to placate me. In the end, she sighed, her eyes cold, her eyebrows furrowed in clear annoyance.

I'll never forget that look in her eyes. The familiar and kind person I had known suddenly felt like a stranger. And then her phone rang. As she took out the phone, her face noticeably brightened.

"Hello, Yeonsoo. Why are you calling?"

I stared at her changed expression in awe. I don't remember exactly how I felt. But that day, I told her that she didn't need to visit anymore.

Hearing that, she brightened again, the same way she had when she had seen who was calling her. She apologized once more for not visiting often and didn't come back for a long, long time.

I kept waiting for her, though. I always stood by the window where I could see the orphanage gates, and I kept checking the mailbox in case she had sent a letter. On the rare occasion that I did receive one, I would read it over and over. Hoping that, one day, she might come back for me.

That wish, which I had long since discarded, was a shameful memory for me.

They hadn't done anything wrong. She and my friend weren't bad people. She had simply been kind to her daughter's friend. I knew that their intentions were good.

But for a long time, I hated them. And I was disgusted with myself for hating them. Because I was still small-minded and immature, this memory still upset me. They might not have done anything wrong, but neither had I. I had simply opened my heart to an adult who was kind to me. And I had wanted a parent. That was all.

If no one did anything wrong, why did it hurt so much?

It had taken far too long for me to finally put aside the question that kept clawing at my heart.

I was exhausted. I had hoped that she, and then my parents from this life, would become my family. But each time, things had gone wrong, and if it happened again, it would be the third time. I was too tattered and too hurt to jump into a new adventure and risk more heartbreak.

Marie and Derick were more important to me than any of the people I had known before. I didn't have the courage to risk being abandoned by them too. I kept telling myself it would be okay, but my anxiety held on to me with a vise-like grip.

You'll be alone forever, it whispered inside me. *No one will ever love you.*

CHAPTER
THIRTY-FIVE

All my hopes had been dashed each time. It was inevitable. Clinging to something I couldn't have would only make things harder for me.

There were some things in this world you just couldn't change. While some people didn't have to do anything to receive love, others could try everything and still not receive even a shred of what everyone else had. I knew that, but...

I, too, wanted a family.

If I was going to be reborn anyway, why couldn't I have been reborn as Marie and Derick's child? Or at least as the heroine, like Rietta. If I were a lovable heroine, would I have been able to become part of the family as easily as Rietta had?

I buried my face in my hands. I couldn't even accept the truth, so giving up was difficult. It all seemed so attainable, just within reach, that I couldn't help but imagine.

If I had been their child, the youngest one, a child who required more attention, who would be more lovable because she was more pitiful. Had there been no other child to be compared to.

That's right. Maybe...

Maybe if you didn't exist...

My train of thought came to a screeching halt as the door was thrown open.

"Wen!"

Green hair flew in the wind, and a fresh scent filled the room. It was Rietta. The lovely, lovable heroine of this world, the girl I had seconds ago wished didn't exist.

Rietta ran over to me. Her smile lit up her face, which had no trace of darkness. I looked at that face in wonder.

"How..."

"Hm?" Rietta was beaming at me, her eyes full of affection and a clueless, bright expression on her face.

"How could I..."

Inferiority, fear, and jealousy—the sharp, pointy feelings I had tried my best to cover up, to ignore, had reared their ugly heads. Her pretty face was so bright and pure, and there was no trace of resentment or hatred. She would never be jealous of me or wish that I didn't exist.

She was such a sweet little sister.

Before I could even try to stop them, tears fell from my eyes. "Rietta..." Through my clouded vision, I saw her consternation.

"Huh? Who did this? Who made you cry?"

"Rietta, you are my little sister."

"Yes, I am. I know. Why?"

"I like you a lot. I love you, my dear sister."

Rietta was my family. And not only her, but Shuell, Derick, Marie, Bessie, and all the other household staff too. Though I couldn't quite believe that they considered me family, to me they were.

"I love you so much, but..."

There was a lump in my throat. When I forced myself to keep talking, more tears streamed down my cheeks.

"W-why did I grow up like this?"

"Wen? What's wrong, Wen?"

"I tried. I tried so, so hard. I wanted to be better. I tried so hard, but I turned out like this anyway."

Rietta, who looked bewildered, pulled me into a tight embrace. She told me not to cry as she awkwardly patted my back, but it made me cry more. I wailed like a child in the arms of my little sister, who was taller than me.

I was jealous of Rietta, didn't trust Marie and Derick, and was envious of Shuell. No matter how much I loved them and how much time passed, I would probably continue to feel that way. They were all perfect, as if they had been born that way, and I couldn't be like that no matter how hard I tried.

I didn't like my biological parents, from both my past life and this one. I'd been exasperated at them and sick of the way they'd acted, and I hated them more than anyone.

But the hardest thing to bear was the fact that I was becoming more like them.

As much as I hated them, it was inevitable that I would become like them. I was their child, after all. The thought made me shudder. I had been disgusted by all the immoral things they had done.

That was why I had really, really tried. Even if nobody acknowledged it, even if it was something I could never tell anyone. I tried everything to become more like the people I loved.

But in the end, it didn't work.

"Nothing changed. Why me? Why am I..."

"Oh no, what's got you so torn up, Wen? Did someone bully you? Should I tell them off?"

"I r-really, really love you, my dear sister. I love you so much. I mean it."

"I know, I know. I love you too, Wen. Don't cry. Shush. What do you need?"

Rietta was kind. She was a lot like Derick, like Marie, like Shuell.

Because they were family.

I loved her very much, but at the same time, I envied her for having something I couldn't have, even though we had started off the same way.

I love you, but I also hate you.

Because she, who was like me, had something I yearned for so much. And while I understood why I couldn't stop myself from hating her, I couldn't stand how disgusted I was by it. I had lived alongside these genuinely wonderful people, doing everything I could to be like them. But in the end, it just wasn't possible.

"You didn't grow up at all, Wen. You're still shorter than I am. You can still grow. It's not too late," Rietta said, doing her best to cheer me up. Her embrace was warm.

You are so strong and kind. I know that wouldn't change even if you knew that I envied you.

Rietta would still treat me like her beloved sister, and she wouldn't regret being so nice to me when we were young. I knew that, and it made me feel more guilty. I loved her all the more for it.

And it made me all the more miserable.

"Are you really not going to tell me why you cried?"

As soon as I had stopped crying, Rietta began to badger

me. She looked worried, and I gave her an awkward smile.

"I might not be able to do much, but I can listen. And I'm perfectly able to punch whoever made you cry a couple of—"

"Rietta."

"Come on, tell me what made you cry!" She pouted, her eyebrows drawing together, but even at the sight of her pleading expression, I kept my mouth shut.

After a brief staring match, Rietta finally let out a sigh. "Fine. I guess you have your reasons. But if you want to talk, I'll be there for you. All right?"

Her words, full of trust and love, felt like a chokehold around my neck. Rietta trusted me, liked me enough to want to spend her time trying to help me. She didn't know the truth about me, about the kind of person I was.

I looked at her with pale nonchalance for a moment and, unable to stop myself said, "No."

"Hmm?"

"I'm not the kind of person you should trust and look up to." It was like a confession. I couldn't hold back the guilt that was consuming me. "I'm not as perfect as you think I am."

Rietta was still looking at me with a puzzled expression. I held back the nausea threatening to overcome me and continued.

"I'm not that compassionate. I'm small-minded and greedy, but I can't even take responsibility for it, and..."

I wanted you to disappear.

I couldn't bring myself to say it. I wanted to relieve some of my guilt without being disliked. How hypocritical.

My face flushed. I opened and closed my mouth a couple of times before I choked out, "Rietta, I... I'm so ashamed of myself."

After I managed to spit out those words, I felt winded, as if I had been running. I felt like a sinner who had just confessed all of her sins.

Then I heard Rietta's voice.

"Well, Wen. That's because..." she said, so casually. "You're not perfect."

As if it was nothing.

"What?" The tears that had threatened to show themselves again immediately retreated.

At my exasperated expression, Rietta kept talking, calmly and coolly. "And that's not because you're different, Wen."

Her answer was so curious that I simply stared at her in a daze.

"Shuell and me, mom and dad—none of us is perfect. We're all ashamed of ourselves every once in a while."

"But I'm much more—"

"I think to myself that I must be the dumbest person alive at least once a day."

My heart sank at her nonchalant declaration. *You? Really?*

"Why would you—"

"...and Wen! All humans are like that."

Just as I was about to get angry at her for not saying so sooner, Rietta cut me off.

"We can't possibly be happy all the time. We cry when we're sad, yell when we're angry, and then, sometimes, something good happens, so we smile." Rietta's tone was perfectly even, as if she hadn't just been worried. It was nearly alarming how unaffected she seemed. "You're really sad and in pain and having a hard time right now, right?"

I nodded without thinking.

Rietta smiled faintly. "That's okay."

Her words filled my head. Like a drop of water falling into a still lake, her words rippled across my heart.

"Just because you're sad right now doesn't mean your world will fall apart tomorrow," she continued, and it was soothing, like a bedtime story read to a child who can't sleep. "If you fail, you can try again. Just because you stumbled doesn't mean you'll fall off a cliff." Not too loud or too quiet, but calm. "I'm not telling you to stop being sad. But I would like you not to despair, Wen."

The emotions all tangled up in a mess inside my heart seemed to unfurl at her next words. "You are an imperfect person, just like everyone else—like me, or Shuell, or the rest—a normal person."

Her voice was even, her words clear, and when I looked at Rietta, I saw her in a new light. It felt odd. Nothing had been resolved. And yet, my heart settled down. As if all those things that had hurt me had never mattered.

Rietta smiled at the face I made. "Although you're still the most beautiful person in the world."

I couldn't help but laugh along with her at her playful declaration. I had just been crying, but it felt like Rietta had cast a spell.

"When did you get so mature?" I muttered, smiling back.

She grinned widely. "You raised me."

I stared at her. Her grin looked like mine.

Once I was done talking to Rietta, I left to find Marie and Derick.

Maybe it was because my heart had settled down and because I had cried for a good while, but it felt as though my mind had been completely overturned. I experienced quite a few new revelations, and that was what I wanted to tell them, but I hadn't expected to start crying again as soon as I walked in.

I dabbed at my eyes and took a deep breath. Why had I cried? I didn't know. Seeing Derick's and Marie's faces just brought back the tears.

They had looked uneasy as they opened the door for me, but their eyes widened at my tears, and they led me to the reception room and gave me time to collect myself, offering me tea and biscuits.

I calmed down after a good long cry, and suddenly felt extremely embarrassed.

"*Hic.*"

One last sob escaped my lips and broke the silence.

When I glanced up, Kendrick sighed deeply.

Hey, what's with the sigh? Can't a person cry every once in a while?

The sudden resentment brought more tears to my eyes. As I started to hold my breath in an attempt to stave them off, Marie got to her feet and stepped closer to me.

"Why won't you stop crying, you little fool?"

Despite the scolding words, her touch was soft. The cuff of her sleeve was rough on my cheeks as she wiped away my tears, despite her trying her best to be gentle. But I didn't push her away.

"Don't cry. Shush."

My vision got blurry again at her words. Why did those words make me cry even more?

"We've thought about it a lot since we parted earlier." Derick's voice was low. I listened to him, letting Marie continue to dab at my face. "We really, really tried our best to raise you well. We loved you a lot."

His words seemed to weigh down my heart.

I know you love me. I really do, more than anyone else.

"But we figured that maybe that wasn't your experience."

I said nothing.

"Wen, did we ever treat you differently?" He asked whether, perhaps, they had treated me differently in some way despite their best efforts, because I was the oldest, and because I wasn't their real daughter.

I slowly shook my head. "No. You always treated me well." It hadn't been their fault. "But, still, I'm not your family, so—"

"It really hurts when you say that, Wen!" Derick's raised voice cut through my mumbling. Startled, I looked up, and I was met with his painful look.

"Had Shuell not proposed to you, we would have officially adopted you long ago."

I was stunned into silence.

"Wen, you are my daughter. Even you can't deny that!" Derick exclaimed as if scolding me.

Marie wrapped an arm around his shoulders and called his name in a soothing voice as he sat there, clearly agitated. He quickly calmed down and blew out a long breath.

"I'm sorry for raising my voice, Wen."

"N-no, I…"

"Do you know how hurt I was? I did everything I could to raise you well and you're here saying we're not family! Honestly!"

I flinched at the barrage of accusations. As I blinked at him, Derick let out another deep sigh.

His words were similar to those he had said on that

cold winter day as he warmed my icy cheeks because I had returned with a reddened nose, having given my scarf to Shuell.

I wasn't scared or sad now.

"I didn't know you felt that way," Marie said in a low voice when Derick went quiet. "I am sorry for letting you believe that, my sweetheart."

Her warm words pained me. *Why are you apologizing to me? You did nothing wrong.* They were not the ones who needed to apologize. And I had already given up on ever getting an apology from those who did.

I had no idea why an apology from someone who didn't owe me one wrenched at my heart.

"Let us get through this together," Derick said as I held back my tears again. "I am sure it will take more than this one time for you to feel better. But let us keep trying together until you do, my child."

I bit down on my lower lip. Derick was right. Though it seemed as though I was much better for now, my old trauma was going to rear its ugly head again. On that day, I was sure to push them away again, saying that we weren't family, and they would get hurt yet again.

"Is that all right?" I asked quietly, and they immediately nodded their heads.

"Yes, of course."

Why are you doing all of this for me? I'm not special, so why?

"We love you very much," Marie said, as if she had heard my thoughts. "Always remember that, Wen. My dear child."

Her words were somehow so firm that they filled me with a strange sense of assurance. It felt as though even if this happened again, it would be all right. I didn't know why, but that's how I felt.

I thought I might cry if I tried to speak, so I just nodded.

The next morning...

I bet my eyes are all puffy. I hadn't looked in the mirror yet, but it was obvious. I took a moment to contemplate as I rubbed my eyelids but decided to tug on the bell pull anyway. It didn't take long for someone to knock at my door.

"My lady, are you... oh, my."

My personal maid, Emily, froze as soon as she cheerfully threw open my bedroom door and stepped inside. I had expected this reaction, so I simply sighed.

"Is it that bad?"

"Yes. It is."

If even Emily was saying that, I really must have looked very terrible. Before I could say anything else, she brought me a cold towel and water to wash my face.

"How unusual. I've never seen you like this, my lady." She sounded the same as usual, but she was using honorifics for once.

"Did you get told off for all that 'little madam' business?" I asked cautiously.

Emily's shoulders sagged almost imperceptibly. Cleaning my face with practiced movements, she replied, "I deserved it."

"Hmm, I guess you did."

Emily didn't narrow her eyes at me or counter my teasing response with a quip of her own. She simply nodded. Then she bowed her head.

"I apologize, my lady."

"Huh?" Emily had always been very polite, but we had become close over the many years we had spent together. I felt flustered at her sudden show of formality. "Why are you acting like this all of a sudden?"

"I thought you didn't want me to be so formal, so I thought I would lighten the mood and make those jokes, but..." She bit her lip. "I deserve to be punished for teasing the lady I serve."

"No, don't do this. I was a bit disappointed, but this isn't like us, Emily." I hurriedly helped Emily to straighten up. Her eyes had gotten teary. Everyone was so tenderhearted.

When I stroked her hair, Emily's brows furrowed even more.

"I'm sorry, my lady."

"I know. It's all right."

"But please, don't leave," she added, as if I was going to disappear at any moment. "I'll try harder to serve you better. Please?"

At her desperate plea, I had to smile. "Even harder, you say?"

"Yes, much more than I do now."

Oh my, how reassuring.

"I seem to have worried quite a few people. I'm all right."

Emily's beseeching gaze didn't change much at my words. Perhaps because I habitually repeated them. I sat there, calmly looking away from her, before speaking up again.

"Actually, I might not be all right." People don't change overnight, after all, and I had just gotten started. "But I'll keep trying to be."

Only then did Emily let out a sigh of relief. "Thank you, my lady."

"I'm doing this for my own good."

"But still."

Emily was stubborn like this sometimes. I stroked the hair of my brusque, sweet personal maid once more and finished washing up.

The weather seemed nice, so I stepped over to the door to crack it open. When I did, I could see a mop of platinum-blond hair through the gap. He jolted as he stepped back, apparently having been leaning against the door.

I tilted my head. "Shuell?"

Before Arwen found Shuell, he had already been standing outside her door, rubbing his face with his hands.

At the Severilous estate, where all the staff were incredibly invested in what was going on, the news of people fighting had spread quickly. Especially since the oldest daughter had been involved.

Arwen had cried and fought with his parents. And Shuell... he hadn't been able to do anything.

Technically, Shuell started all of this. His proposal had set everything in motion. It could have concluded as merely a ridiculous incident in which Arwen was left dumbfounded and Shuell a little hurt. But it had blown up completely out of proportion.

The staff of the Severilous household, who were

invested, but also particularly good at keeping secrets, had let him know that Arwen had cried but had not explained why exactly. Rietta had told Shuell only one thing.

"Wen must have gone through a lot because of us."

Shuell, who was pretty quick on the uptake, could tell what that meant. Wen usually acted as though nothing was wrong, but at times she would be in a mood that was hard to describe. He realized that his actions had opened Arwen's long-ignored wounds and brought them to light. And he had since been lost in numerous bouts of self-reflection and loathing.

This had happened a few times during Shuell's lengthy period of unrequited love. His desire for Arwen not to be hurt was as strong as his love for her. Because he loved her, he couldn't put his feelings above her well-being. Shuell really tried. That was why he had never leered at her or tried to awkwardly flirt with her.

But he had confessed because he couldn't hide his feelings for her forever. It was simply a confession. Not a terrible public proposal. Just the truth.

He hadn't pressured Arwen to feel the same. They were her feelings, after all. It wasn't as though begging would make her reciprocate his affection. Having spent such a long time loving her, Shuell had gotten used to the unrequited nature of his feelings. But still...

He just wanted her to let him keep his feelings. He didn't want anything from her. He only wanted her to know. But if even that was uncomfortable, then...

The right thing to do is to give up.

They said little strokes fell great oaks, but Arwen was a person, not a tree. All these years, Shuell had done his best to ensure that Arwen didn't feel overwhelmed, and she had never said that he made her uncomfortable. But what if she had only been enduring it this whole time?

I should give up.

Shuell came to this conclusion almost immediately. But at the same time, the very thought pained him. His unrequited love had persevered because he had told himself that he didn't need it to be reciprocated and that he didn't mind getting rejected.

Shuell stood in front of Arwen's bedroom door and leaned his forehead against it.

He was only startled for a moment when the door opened—and he heard her gentle voice. The voice he loved more than everything else.

"Shuell?"

He quickly showed her a radiant smile. "Hi, Wen."

His worries faded away as if they had never mattered. For Shuell, it was inevitable. Feelings of resentment at having his affections ignored began to form at times. But whenever he faced her, none of that mattered.

So, he should be fine.

I should be able to stop loving you for your sake, because I love you so much.

CHAPTER
THIRTY-SEVEN

Shuell turned around to face me. His expression, which had looked conflicted, brightened into a beaming smile, but then fell again.

I chuckled, his face calling to mind a crestfallen puppy. I knew why Shuell had come to see me.

He was hesitant to speak first and eyed me warily. I led him into my room, sat him down, and served him some tea.

"You heard, didn't you?" I said.

Shuell coughed on the sip of tea he had taken. I grinned at the sight. He wiped his mouth and looked at me like a puppy who knew he was in trouble.

"I'm sorry." He didn't hesitate to apologize. He was always like this, but even more so today. "I didn't intend to, but everyone was acting all strange, so I asked one of the staff members what had happened. They told me that they had teased you and that... you hadn't been happy about it at all."

I guess that's what everyone is saying. It wasn't entirely untrue.

"It's my fault. I was careless. I'm sorry." Shuell looked

even more solemn than usual. He must have been feeling really guilty. His usually pink eyes seemed darker with sorrow.

I stared at him for a moment. If this had been before I had fought with Marie and Derick, I would have thrown a fit at Shuell's words. But the issue had been brought up because of that fight.

I reached a simple conclusion. "It's not your fault."

Shuell looked up at me in doubt, and I gave him a bright smile. I felt sorry for myself and loathed myself in equal measure, and Shuell had initiated it all. There was more than enough reason to be angry, and he was kind enough to bear my excessive fury. The Shuell I knew wasn't someone who put himself above the comfort of others. The staff had made a fuss, but I knew that Shuell hadn't intended for that to happen.

Because I felt so sorry for myself and didn't have enough emotional capacity to care about others, I could have blamed him. And he would have taken it all without saying a word, not daring to even try to argue. But this wasn't anybody's fault. There had just been a bit of disharmony caused by a slight mismatch in everyone's expectations.

"You know that," I said evenly.

"Wen," Shuell interjected. His brows were furrowed as if this upset him more than me. Though I tended to fear people who furrowed their eyebrows, he was one of the few people I didn't fear.

Why does he look sad rather than angry when he furrows his eyebrows like that? As I contemplated this petty thought, Shuell spoke up again.

"I started it. If I hadn't prepared such a ridiculous proposal, this wouldn't have happened. You're right, Wen. I should have thought about what position I, we, are in."

It was true. Our social status dictated that even liking someone could be interpreted in many ways.

Shuell smiled, but he still looked sad. "If I hadn't made my feelings obvious, no... if I hadn't liked you in the first place..." His voice got quieter as he spoke. But his words were clear.

Having listened to him calmly, I put down my teacup. The *clink* it made sounded cold. The tea I hadn't even touched was no longer warm.

"So... are you trying to apologize for doing something wrong, or are you trying to get me to vent my anger at you?" My tone was as cold as the tea.

Shuell's eyes grew wide. His face looked vulnerable and frail, as if any biting remark would leave a scar.

"It's not your fault that I fought with your parents. Your actions might have triggered it, but it would have happened sooner or later anyway."

Shuell didn't reply.

"Do you think your love is wrong?" I continued. "The love you have nurtured for over ten years, according to you? Why is it suddenly wrong now?"

Shuell smiled as if he was embarrassed at my pointed reproach. I pressed my lips together, harder, because it looked as though he was shrugging it off.

"Of course not. I know you. I know better than anyone that you are not capable of being that selfish. Even now, you're making a face like you're ready to take back your affections if they inconvenienced me in any way. You were the same when we were younger."

Despite my barrage of sharp words, Shuell kept smiling, a smile that meant that he knew he had done wrong but was too stubborn to change.

I let out a deep sigh. "You just want me to lash out at you."

Shuell's eyes widened again, and he waved his hands in denial. It didn't convince me at all.

"Is that why you're here? Did you think I would be grateful to have someone to chew out and start shouting at you?"

"No. That's not it." He shook his head.

I bit my lip in frustration. He was watching me cautiously, clearly taken aback by my reaction. It would have been better if he had actually done something wrong and refused to admit it. I hated seeing him all despondent over something that wasn't even his fault.

This wasn't the first time, either. Shuell often acted this way. He was kind to everyone, and especially to me. He would get flustered if he ever did anything slightly wrong and be hyperaware of how he treated and spoke to me.

Because he liked me.

I wasn't grateful for it at all.

"Shuell. I don't like that you act submissive toward me just because you like me."

I liked Shuell. Not the way he liked me, but I cared for him just as much as I did Rietta, and it pained me to think about the way he was pining after me. I wanted him to like someone who could give him love the way he did, not just receive his love. There were plenty of relationships he could get into where he wouldn't have to be submissive—but could stand as an equal.

Why do you have to like someone like me? You could do so much better.

"I really thought I had done something wrong. But Wen, you barely ever get angry and always suppress your feelings." I tried to hold back my anguish as Shuell said softly, "I was trying to be considerate, but that might not be how you see it. Everyone makes sense of things differently."

Shuell trailed off and twiddled his thumbs. His face looked dejected. *Hmm.*

"So, I thought that maybe my feelings had affected you negatively, but you hadn't been able to say anything because you were trying to be considerate."

His pitiful words rendered me speechless. It wasn't because he was accurate or because I found his concern commendable, but because I was a bit exasperated. How weak did he think I was?

"Shuell, this is a little embarrassing."

Shuell tipped his head to the side in confusion.

I grimaced. "Do you think I'm some kind of fragile dried flower that gets crushed if you hold it too tightly?"

It had been thirteen long years. He thought I hadn't been able to say anything that whole time because I was afraid I might hurt his feelings?

How fragile does he think my heart is? Or does he think I'm that patient?

"I am neither that generous nor frail. Even if I had tried to be considerate, it couldn't have lasted more than a year. I would have endured it for that long and then told you that I was really sorry, but could you please stop because it's killing me."

Shuell seemed slightly stunned by my harsh words. I let out a long breath before continuing.

"Your feelings have never inconvenienced me. They never caused me any sort of trouble, nor got others involved, and I've almost never felt conflicted because of you."

His expression looked both relieved and troubled at the same time. I had thought he would be happy, so this was unexpected.

"What is it?"

"Nothing. I'm glad you weren't inconvenienced, but..." Shuell looked even more troubled now. His gaze was fixed downward as his lips formed unspoken words. Then he raised his head again. "...shouldn't you have felt a little conflicted?"

"About what?"

"No, I mean... Of course, I don't want you to suffer or anything. But... usually, when someone confesses their feelings, you shouldn't be completely unaffected, right?"

Shuell looked confused now. It seemed hard for him to continue, but he said, "I have liked you for a long time, Wen. And I thought it was obvious. Did it really not affect you at all?"

Shuell tended to wear his heart on his sleeve. Even now, his sadness was evident. His eyebrows drooped, and his eyes glistened.

I finally understood what he meant.

For people to truly connect, such conflict was necessary. If Shuell's feelings were to be reciprocated, I should have been affected by them, and he was disappointed to hear that I hadn't been. If the person you liked had no feelings for you whatsoever, and there was no hope for any to ever arise, it meant that your love would be forever unrequited.

This is good. It is better for Shuell to give up.

But... honestly?

"Shu, I really didn't want to say this, in case I was giving you too much hope." I had a lot to say when it came to this particular matter. "Don't you think you're being a bit cowardly?"

CHAPTER
THIRTY-EIGHT

Shuell looked surprised by my seemingly unrelated comment. It was evident that he had no idea what I was talking about, which was frustrating.

"Look, Shuell," I said firmly. "You like me, but I don't like you the way you do, right?"

He nodded almost reflexively. Even as I was talking, I wondered whether I should be telling him this, but I couldn't stop myself.

"So, what would you have to do to get what you want?"

"Wen." His expression hardened suddenly, and his eyebrows drew together. I hardly ever saw such an angry look on his face. "Get what I want? People aren't objects—"

"Yes, I agree. But this is life, and a little bit of rule-breaking is necessary sometimes. Of course, you can't kidnap someone to try and win over their heart, but shouldn't there be *some* wooing involved?"

The prim and proper Shuell still seemed to disapprove of my choice of words, but he nodded.

"Think about it, though," I continued. "Did you ever try

to woo me?”

It was true. If you sat around waiting for someone to notice you, what were your chances of catching their attention? I could swear, in my eleven years at the Academy, Shuell had never once tried. Confessing, sure—he had confessed to me so many times that I was sick of it. But that was it.

“You say you like me, but it doesn’t seem like I make your heart flutter. You smile at me a lot, but you’re always smiling.”

Shuell opened his mouth as if to argue, but I kept up the flood of words, not letting him voice his opinion.

“‘I like you,’ ‘I like you,’ over and over again. You kept saying it as if you were memorizing it for an exam. How is that supposed to make me feel anything?”

It might have been different if I had liked him in that way too. But to me, Shuell was just a boy I happened to be close to. No more, no less. If he wanted to change my perspective, he needed to put in some effort. More than just constantly confessing his affections.

Once I was done talking, I crossed my arms and eyed him.

“I was being considerate!” he said in a raised voice, apparently feeling wronged.

“How?”

"What was I supposed to do, take your hand and kiss you without your consent—even though I know full well that you're not interested in me? Make it obvious in front of everyone that I like you and treat you like we're a couple?"

I blinked. *Hmm, I suppose not. That would be bad.*

"I know you didn't believe my confessions for a long time, Wen. But wouldn't you have been overwhelmed if I had made it really obvious?"

He wasn't wrong. Shuell's expression was downcast as he voiced his objections, sounding frustrated, and I felt a bit sorry for him. But at the same time, I couldn't understand him. I hesitated before speaking again.

"So, you're all right with me not liking you back?"

"No! Of course, I want you to like me back!"

That was so loud. I winced. And at the same time, I found it even harder to understand what he was saying.

"Then what were you thinking, just sitting around and not doing anything?"

"I told you. I didn't do anything because I knew it'd make you uncomfortable."

"Still, you can't expect something to happen without even trying anything..." I said in exasperation.

Shuell let out an embarrassed laugh. "That's true," he readily agreed. But he seemed so forlorn, and it was upsetting.

What was I even trying to say? *"I don't like you. But that's probably because you didn't even try to flirt with me."* Was I saying that I would fall for him if he did?

I chewed on my bottom lip. I couldn't be sure that I wouldn't. Really, I had no idea. If Shuell started flirting with me, would I be able to keep my heart from fluttering?

Falling in love didn't require some dramatic event or fate. People fell in love at the incidental touch of a hand or because of a few overlapping coincidences. If Shuell really went for it, I might fall for him after only a few gestures and meaningful glances.

But at the same time, if my heart was that fickle, I had no way of knowing it wouldn't fall for someone else just as easily, or how long my love would last. My love wasn't that grand. Unlike Shuell, who had loved me for a very long time and had suppressed his own desires for my sake.

"Why were you so considerate towards me?" It would've been better if he had been more selfish. If he had pushed his feelings on me regardless of what I wanted, I could have at least rejected him much more easily. "Are you fine with the way things are?"

I'd thought he was fickle. Like the sunlight on a spring day, I thought he liked me without much forethought at all. Even when he tried his best to express his feelings to me, I kept doubting them. I would never be able to love as deeply as he did. But if his feelings for me were that deep, how did he endure all those years of not having them reciprocated?

I don't think I'll ever be able to love you as much as you love me, so is it really okay for you to keep loving me?

The words I wanted to say were on the tip of my tongue before I swallowed them back down. I still wondered whether it was okay for me to say these things. I didn't want to give him false hope.

Shuell didn't answer right away. He watched me with a strange expression before grinning.

I shouldn't have asked it. Of course, he'd say that it was okay.

Shuell Severilous, you kind fool.

"You think too much, Wen."

I grimaced at his unexpected remark. "What?"

"It's simple, right? You just have to worry about your own feelings. If you like me, then you can accept my feelings, and if not, you can tell me to stop because it's annoying and makes you uncomfortable."

His pink eyes sparkled. They were ridiculously bright. I let out a huff of exasperation.

"Is that how you stopped yourself from even touching me this whole time?"

We're the same in the end—you and I. We both loved each other very much, though in different ways. In the same way I worried about him, he had done nothing more than make confessions to me and otherwise keep his love to himself. But that was why I worried about him. If this continued, I suspected I'd continue worrying about him.

"Right. Honestly... it's not like there's zero possibility. I never thought of you as just my younger brother." I paused for a moment, feeling oddly frustrated, and finally let out a long exhale. I had no idea if this was the right thing to do. I really didn't know.

But something had to change between us, for better or worse. We couldn't stay like this forever.

"This whole time, I thought we could never become a family. Everyone at the estate is so wonderful, and I'm not."

"Wen! That's—"

"Settle down," I interrupted. Shuell had predictably raised his voice at my words. "I've decided to work on it. Anyway, that's why I never thought of you as just my younger brother." I took a deep breath. "But that doesn't mean that I will certainly fall for you. Does that make sense?"

This was the best I could do. It was a vague answer, but at least it wasn't a lie.

Shuell acted as if he wasn't in pain, but there was no way

he wasn't. How much more pain would he have to endure because of me? I almost wanted to accept his feelings, even if I had to lie. But if I did, I knew that one day he would realize the truth and be devastated.

My final offer was more like the lesser evil than the best option.

"I know I might be giving you false hope. But I don't want to deceive you," I added hurriedly, before biting my lip. It sounded like an excuse, no matter how you looked at it.

"Wen."

When I didn't meet his eyes, Shuell got out of his seat and went down on one knee in front of me.

"Please look at me."

I couldn't avoid his gaze any longer. I reluctantly met his eyes and was taken aback. He was smiling broadly. As always, it was a beautiful smile. A smile only Shuell could make.

"That's all I needed." His soothing voice sounded almost like a song. "You don't have to force yourself to try and accept my feelings. It's enough that I can keep my feelings for you, Wen."

He carefully took my hand in his. It was a soft, light touch, easy enough to swat away if I wanted to. I looked down at Shuell, who was gingerly holding my hand, as if handling something fragile and precious.

"I'm very patient. I'm good at suppressing my feelings and waiting. If you had only ever seen me as a younger brother, I might have been a little sad, but…"

Though it had started off strong, Shuell's voice trailed off. He leaned his forehead against my knees. A moment of silence passed.

"I'm just glad you don't hate me." His quiet voice trembled a little. I couldn't see his face because he had his head lowered, but I could hear the relief in his tone. "Will you give me one more chance then, Wen?"

I didn't reply.

"I'll try harder." When he raised his head, he was smiling again, and I stared at his radiant face.

How come your smile is so pretty?

Shuell's love was deeper than I could possibly fathom. He had spent so much of his feelings on me already, but he was acting all energetic—as if he had plenty more to spare. His golden hair glittered in the sunlight as he lowered his face again.

He was so beautiful. How could a boy so pretty have fallen for me?

Feeling a familiar sense of pity, I raised my hand and stroked his hair. It wasn't as fluffy as it had been when he was younger, but it was still as soft.

I asked a familiar question. "Do you like me that much?"

Shuell raised his head. "Yes, I do."

It was a familiar reply. Not a sign of hesitation.

"I like you *very*, very much."

It was strange, and I couldn't understand it, but...

As always, it was a lovely reply.

CHAPTER
THIRTY-NINE

I didn't sleep well that night.

For no particular reason, I felt uneasy and restless, and whenever I did manage to fall asleep, my dreams would be just as unsettling. Shuell in tears, heartbroken. Shuell, watching me nervously. Shuell, forcing a smile as he told me he was fine.

Visions of Shuell plagued my dreams.

But ironically, the last dream I had that night was of him smiling brightly. We were in a sunlit garden, and he was leaning down to meet my gaze as he smiled his slightly mischievous smile. He kissed the back of my hand, almost reverently, and looked up at me, beaming.

"I like you, Wen."

The subconscious was so easily affected. I figured this happened because I had been thinking about Shuell and confessions all night before finally falling asleep.

Thanks to this dream, I woke even before the sun came up, and I had to fight the urge to go and disturb Shuell's sleep by stealing his warm blankets. Though the world may have seemed to fall apart yesterday, today the sun rose again. I was tired from barely getting any sleep and my mind was filled with chaotic thoughts, but I had duties to take care of.

In other words, I had to go to work.

As I stepped into the carriage that would take me to the royal palace, the thought crossed my mind: *I wish I could just quit.* I only had one day off a week, and that was yesterday. It was human nature to want to rest more, even after a break; Mondays had been the worst days in my past life.

It wouldn't really matter if I quit...

In the kingdom, you were considered an adult at nineteen, but you didn't graduate from the Academy until you turned twenty. During the final year of schooling, the eleventh year, students chose their own classes and decided on a career path. Academic work suited me, and many had recommended that I become a scholar. But instead, I became a secretary in the Royal Ministry.

Being a scholar meant chasing dreams and a particular field of study. In this world, it wasn't uncommon for nobles to become scholars, but they were fully sponsored by their families. If I had wanted to be a scholar, the Severilous family would have sponsored me, but at the time of my graduation, I'd wanted to avoid being a burden. I'd wanted to earn money so I could move out, and a stable civil service job was great for that. That had been my intention.

I didn't particularly like working at the palace. It wasn't terrible, but I wasn't devoted to it, and it didn't give me any sense of accomplishment either. If I'd had a different job lined up, I would have quit.

Not that I want to be a scholar.

Money wasn't the most important thing, but it was necessary to afford a living. Living a life with someone else's money meant putting your life in their hands. Maybe I should ask if I could become a retainer of the Severilous family. I had experience working as a secretary in the Royal Ministry, and working for the family didn't sound so bad.

"We've arrived, Lady Broschte."

The horseman's call woke me from my musing. Feeling a bit shaken, I contemplated what he had said.

Broschte. That's right...

"Thank you very much, sir," I said to the horseman.

"There's no need to speak formally to me," he replied.

"I prefer it that way."

I usually used the Severilous family carriage, but I hired a separate one to take me to the palace whenever I went to work. I may have been staying at the Severilous mansion, but using the family crest was a completely different matter. My contract with the last horseman had ended, and the new one

I'd hired wasn't used to being spoken to so formally either. And whenever I said it was fine, he would look at me with wide, grateful eyes.

"Th-thank you." He bowed.

I looked at him with an uncomfortable smile. It was strange enough to receive a bow from someone at least ten years older than me, but the other nobles entering the palace were also starting to shoot glances at us. I was a noble who used formal language when talking to commoners. I never dropped formalities unless we were close, and I never treated them badly. This did not reflect particularly well on me.

If I had been a high-ranking noble, speaking formally to those of a lower status may have been regarded in a positive light. It would have been the ideal picture of a benevolent superior, though of course there would still be concerns about blurring the lines between social classes. But I was the daughter of the Broschte viscounty, which was all but gone, and nobility only in name. My using formal language with commoners didn't make me look like a benevolent noble, but rather as if I was on the same level as they were, only a noble in appearance.

I was well aware of this. But I didn't want to change my behavior. I had lived in a world where all humans were supposed to be equal, and I believed that to be moral. No matter their social class or job, they were human, just like me. I had no desire to look down on someone simply because the unjust customs of this world had put me in a superior position.

As I stepped out of the carriage and headed into the palace, I could feel several eyes fixed on me. An elderly noblewoman clicked her tongue in disapproval as she walked past me. I kept my expression neutral as I ignored her. I was used to it already, and I didn't intend to pay attention to the numerous microaggressions I faced each day. I was right about this, and they were wrong. And more importantly...

They all said it was all right.

The Severilouses had always been kind to their household servants. It was why I had been fairly certain it would be all right for me to share my opinions on this matter. But at the same time, I had been scared. After all, they had grown up in a world with a class system and had known nothing else. But they had accepted my views without judgment. In the same way they had adopted Rietta as their daughter, even though she had been a commoner, they had embraced me wholeheartedly.

"The majority isn't always correct. This must have been hard for you to bear alone, Wen. You did well. We're proud of you."

I almost came to a halt then and there as I got choked

up. Since my argument with Marie and Derick, memories of them showing me their love kept cropping up. I was sure those days had gone by without me taking notice. But looking back now, I felt like I really had been loved, and that was a strange thought.

I took a deep breath and slowly continued walking. When I arrived at the office, some of the others had already arrived and were sitting at their desks. I greeted Earl Garden, my superior, before sitting down at my own desk. No one greeted me, and I didn't greet anyone else.

The palace was my workplace. Quite literally, it was a place where I worked, nothing more. Most of the other nobles had no intention of befriending me. I once had a few friends at the Academy, but things changed once I graduated. At the Academy, I was the girl who was sponsored by the Severilous dukedom and close to its two heirs. Thanks to this connection, my own family name hadn't been much of an issue. Sponsorships, however, usually ended upon graduation.

I hadn't joined the Severilous staff as a retainer, nor had I chosen to become a scholar, which would have implied continued support by the dukedom. Neither did it seem like there was anything going on between Shuell and me, so many of the nobles assumed that my connection with the Severilous family had come to an end.

Many of the other secretaries at the palace were older than I was, and since we hadn't been at the Academy at the same time, we didn't have any connections. And because they assumed I was no longer sponsored by the Severilouses, they ignored me. It was not that they disliked me. They just had no reason to befriend me.

Of course, this was conjecture on my part, and it was possible that they actively disliked me—since my status meant that they could do so without consequence. For two years, I'd worked amid this complete disinterest. It didn't really bother me, as they weren't openly bullying or antagonizing me because of my lower status.

I let out a sigh as I organized the work that I had to do that day. This was all inconsequential. It had been ordinary everyday life for the past two years. But for some reason, I suddenly felt lonely in the office where nobody greeted me.

I want to go home.

I wanted to go home, find Derick or Marie, and get a warm, reassuring hug.

If I whine a little about nobody talking to me at the palace, would they take my side?

My vision went blurry. I hurriedly wiped away the tears before they could drop onto the documents. I wasn't usually such a crybaby, but I had been crying a lot the past few days.

Things had been different ever since I cried my eyes out after the fight with Marie and Derick. I couldn't bring myself to call them my parents yet, but something had definitely changed. It had been years since I had become an adult, but it felt like I was a child again.

Blaming them for how emotional I was being, I was shuffling some documents when the office door opened with a knock.

"Excuse me," said a cheerful voice. "I have some documents to deliver." A red-haired young woman entered. I reflexively turned my head toward her but quickly lost interest. People often came by the office.

"Arwen!"

I only looked up again when I heard someone call me excitedly. The red-haired young lady was looking at me with a bright smile. I drew my eyebrows together imperceptibly. Did I know her?

It wasn't an entirely unfamiliar face. It felt like I had seen her somewhere before. But she definitely wasn't someone close enough to me to call me by my first name so casually.

"Don't you remember me? It's Evelyn. Evelyn Kesset. We took kingdom history class together."

Oh. Only then did I recall who she was. The second daughter of the Kesset earldom, a family distinguished for its many famous musicians. She had fiery red hair and was a year younger than I was.

But the smile I was showing her was still strained. Evelyn and I had only ever greeted each other a few times in the hallway. Why was she acting like we were close?

"Goodness, it's been so long. I heard you were working at the palace after you graduated, and it's true! Have you been well?"

"Of course. How about you, Evelyn? I apologize for not recognizing you right away."

"No problem! Unlike you, I wasn't that popular at the Academy, so it's totally understandable."

A look of disappointment briefly crossed Evelyn's face, but she continued chattering away cheerily. Some of the other secretaries began shooting glances in our direction, and I started to get a little annoyed.

Why was she acting like we were friends all of a sudden, especially here at my workplace?

"Evelyn, I'm working right now, so—"

"Oh, right. I'll be making my debut at the harvest festival," Evelyn interrupted my gentle attempt to get her to stop. She looked at me with sparkling eyes, ready to take me by the hand at any moment. "Will you be debuting at the harvest festival as well, Arwen?"

CHAPTER FORTY

My smile turned rigid. I realized why Evelyn had suddenly shown up and acted as though we were friends.

Evelyn had either missed the change in my expression or had chosen to ignore it. "You're really late, you know. Ladies usually make their debut right after graduation, and it's been two years already. But I'm glad that we will be debuting together."

Evelyn was right. Most young noble ladies made their debut in high society right after they graduated, but I hadn't. I had figured I wouldn't need to enter high society anyway.

Things were different now. It was still awkward, but I was planning on doing my best to accept Marie and Derick as my parents. They might adopt me, or... this was less likely, but I might also become the next lady of the Severilous family. Whichever way it went, I would need to become an official part of the Severilous family, so I would have to make my debut as soon as possible.

"The duke will be your chaperone, right? Goodness me. Countless young ladies have asked him to be their chaperone, but he has always refused! I envy you so much."

Her reaction wasn't surprising, but I wasn't entirely happy about it. It meant that she was clearly one of the few nobles who still assumed that I was going to be staying at the Severilous estate long-term.

Evelyn's voice must have been loud enough to overhear—because I could sense several gazes pointed toward us. They must have heard her mention the duke. I showed her my practiced smile.

"Calm down, Evelyn. Nothing has been decided yet."

"But—"

"And this doesn't seem like the proper time or place to discuss this."

Evelyn pouted, her eyebrows drooping in a pitiful, lovely way. "All right. Then let's talk some other time. Will you invite me to the Severilous mansion?"

I kept smiling.

How shameless of you. Just because you sound all cheerful and nice doesn't mean I'll do as you say, little lady.

"I'm not sure. I was going to invite some old friends from the Academy sometime, but because we haven't decided on a date yet, I'm not sure when I'll be free. We wouldn't want our plans to conflict," I said in an apologetic tone. Evelyn's face froze. I smiled gently as I got to my feet. "I can't escort you very far since I'm working, but I'll walk you to the door."

"Oh, all right…"

Evelyn's voice showed her displeasure. I kept smiling, acting as if I hadn't noticed at all, and walked her to the door slowly, stopping there.

"It was nice to see you. Goodbye."

"So that chatterbox finally reached out to you, hmm?"

It was lunchtime, and Sia, who had called me out for a picnic in one of the gardens that were rarely frequented, said this with a knowing shake of her head. Her words were sharp, but her hands were busily opening a picnic basket and taking out sandwiches, juice, and a salad. Sia had invited Elvine and me to have a picnic outside, which was unusual. She acted like she was the most unfriendly person out of all three of us, but she was clearly the most sensitive.

I nodded and took a bite out of a sandwich. "Is she well known? Oh, Sia, this…"

"What? Is it good?" Sia looked at me expectantly.

I chewed on a big mouthful. It tasted like it had been made by a five-year-old who had done their best. It looked delicious, but the bread felt as though it had been kneaded maybe three times.

I'm so glad Sia is not a pâtissier.

"Yes... it's not bad."

Feeling that she might take away my food if I didn't keep my honest opinion to myself, I kept my mouth shut.

Thanks to Sia dragging us here with the promise of a wonderful lunch, there wasn't enough time to go back to the mansion now or ask the servants to bring us another meal. Eating a sandwich that had at least been made with love was better than starving. Besides, the pudding she had brought for dessert looked promising.

"Right? I'm quite skilled, you know."

"Yes. It's good. So, is she popular?"

Sia nodded as she took a bite of her own sandwich. It seemed to taste fine to her. Elvine was taking tiny little bites of her food next to us. I pushed the quiche, which had clearly been made by the Alfredo family chef, over to Elvine as I looked at Sia.

"Evelyn Kesset is the premier source of gossip among social circles. She's so good at spreading gossip that most people think of her rather than her older sister when a daughter of the Kesset family is mentioned. No one really likes her, but because she has so much useful information, it's best to be on friendly terms with her."

Wow. I was impressed. "How do you know all that?

You're amazing."

"This is basic knowledge if you want to survive in high society. You have to keep up with the news, Wen." After telling me off needlessly, Sia finished the last bite of her sandwich. "Anyway, don't be too harsh. It might have been all right until now, but not anymore—"

"Hmm?"

"What?"

"What do you mean, not anymore?"

Sia's eyes widened. She seemed as confused as I was. "What kind of question is that? Aren't you planning on making your debut?"

"Who told you that?" I asked without hiding my annoyance. I had thought about making my debut, but I hadn't told anyone about it, and I didn't like that she was talking about it as if it had already been decided.

Sia shook her head. "No one did. But I'm sure everyone is expecting you to."

"But why?"

"Because it's been two years since you graduated. It's not like you won't debut at all, so this year is your last chance."

Having thought about not debuting at all, I blinked at Sia's words. I hadn't known there was a deadline. Then again, I supposed I hadn't heard of older ladies making their debut.

"Duchess and Duke Severilous wouldn't let you debut at any old ball, so I assumed it would be at the harvest festival. I didn't hear it from anyone, I swear." Sia's voice grew quieter as she talked. By the time she finished her sentence, she was watching me warily, which made me sigh.

"It's fine. Sorry for reacting so aggressively."

Sia's expression softened. I watched her as she wiped some crumbs off Elvine's cheek, looking much more comfortable, and got lost in thought.

I suppose I have to make my debut. It seems like the best time too.

I could already tell how bothersome things were going to get. The harvest festival would be full of other nobles like Evelyn, trying to figure out whether or not I had gotten kicked out of the Severilous house. If conversations like the one I had with Evelyn continued, it would get uncomfortable. I didn't particularly want to see the people who had been ignoring me all this time suddenly play nice with me, either.

"Maybe I should hurry up and quit…"

Thud.

I had been mumbling to myself when I heard the small noise. I looked around. Elvine, who had been eating a sandwich, was staring at me in astonishment mid-chew.

"W-Wen, you're going to quit?"

"Mm. I'm considering it."

"That's a great idea!" Sia exclaimed, beaming, before Elvine could respond. She thwacked my back enthusiastically. It really hurt.

"Do you know how bad I felt for you when you said you'd be working at the palace after graduating? And at the Royal Ministry at that. It would have been a different story if you had said you would become the head maid at the palace because you were ambitious. As a secretary, you just sit around in a stuffy office all day, doing paperwork."

Her flood of words seemed to indicate how long she had been holding back. Sia had always encouraged me to do whatever I set my mind on. She must have been really worried about me.

"I'm not quitting because I have another job lined up or anything. You always overestimate me, Sia," I said.

"Why, then?" Elvine's gray eyes were already filled with tears.

"I thought I might work as a retainer for the Severilous estate."

Elvine looked as though her world was ending. She hesitated before mumbling, "I want to quit too."

"What?"

"I'll be all alone at the palace."

I smiled uneasily as I looked at Elvine, who had put down her sandwich as if she had lost her appetite. Unlike me, who could quit at any time, Elvine didn't have that choice. As the kingdom's only sorceress, she was bound by duty. The king had even created a new office branch called the Magic Department to bring Elvine into the palace as soon as she graduated. She couldn't just quit.

I was patting Elvine's shoulder in an attempt to comfort her when Sia let out a huff of exasperation. "Hey! What about me? Do you know how many times I visited you at the palace even though I don't work here?"

"You... you're..." Elvine stuttered, then finally turned her head away. "You're different..."

It was a simple answer, very characteristic of Elvine, who wasn't one for long explanations. Sia, flushed at the many words left unsaid, snatched the sandwich out of Elvine's hands. Elvine's shoulders drooped.

"I'll visit often, all right?" I tried to comfort Elvine, but she only managed to nod, still looking glum.

CHAPTER
FORTY-ONE

I had pretty much made up my mind, but I couldn't quit my job at the palace right away. I also hadn't gotten rid of the small house I had found for myself. It was kind of like a safety net for the anxiety that was still very much within me.

Marie and Derick had told me that I was their daughter, but I still felt anxious at times. On days like that, I would look at the deed to the small house while feeling a bit pathetic.

Still, I was doing my best to accept that I really was part of the family. For example...

"Wen, you should debut this—"

"Yes, I'm thinking of debuting at the harvest festival."

...by doing this sort of thing.

Dinnertime was when everyone relaxed in perfect harmony. As we waited for dessert amid the gentle atmosphere, Derick cautiously brought up the topic, and I announced my plans.

The dining room went quiet at my nonchalant declaration. I fixed my gaze on my plate, avoiding the sets of eyes looking at me.

"Really?" Marias was the first to speak. Her tone was as flat as ever, but I could tell that she was excited. Marias preferred to listen to her family members talking at the dinner table rather than speaking up herself, so her being the first one to respond was uncommon.

"Yes. I have to debut in high society at some point, after all."

"You don't have to if you don't want to." Even as she said it, there was a faint smile on Marias' lips.

I flashed her a brilliant smile of my own. "No, really. It's all right."

"Wen, if you feel like I'm pressuring you to do it, you don't have to. Just do whatever you like, all right?" Derick chimed in, also looking both worried and overjoyed.

I shook my head. "I came to the conclusion on my own. Even if I don't show my face in high society very often, it would be better to debut. As a… member of the Severilous family, it wouldn't make sense for me not to make my debut." I muttered the last part quietly. I should've said it with more confidence, but I felt uncertain. I took a sip of water to avoid their gazes, and when I put down my glass, the dining room had gone quiet once more.

"Wen…"

Oh no, Derick's crying. I wanted to get up and hug him or

something, but the table was so long that it would have taken forever to reach him.

"D-don't cry."

"I'm not crying. Why would I cry?"

Derick, it's not very convincing when you say that while dabbing at your eyes.

But I kept my mouth shut, and the atmosphere grew even more solemn. Even Marie was avoiding my gaze. I started to feel even more uncertain. *Is this all it takes for them to be so moved? Have I been that... cold?*

But my conflicted feelings disappeared without a trace at Derick's next words. "My dear, I will make sure this will be the best debutante ball."

I felt a peculiar sense of foreboding hanging over me. "Th-thank you."

"You will be the first debutante in this generation of the Severilous family, so everything has to be perfect. It's *your* debut, after all. The harvest festival, you say? That's perfect. You will be the queen of the ball."

I was alarmed. The harvest festival, along with the foundation festival in spring, was the biggest ball in the kingdom, where countless young noble ladies made their debut into high society. I really didn't want to take the spotlight at a huge event like that.

"We must have a dress made for you right away. I should contact Madam Louise. If we don't hurry, we won't be able to get an appointment."

"That won't be a problem, Derick," Marias said. "There's nothing we can't make happen."

"You're right, Marie. Didn't you mention that an unusually large topaz was found at one of our mines? But we already sent it off for auction, didn't we?"

"If you need it, I'll get it back."

A warm, yet oddly scary, conversation went on between the two. I took a nervous bite of the opera cake served for dessert before carefully raising my hand.

"You don't have to do all that—"

"This is the bare minimum, Wen."

Eep!

Marias, whom I had never in my life witnessed raising her voice, was speaking a bit louder than usual. I closed my mouth obediently.

Shuell chuckled sympathetically and patted the back of my hand. "It doesn't seem like they'd stop even if you tried."

"Sadly, no."

Having lost all motivation at Shuell's words, I turned my attention to the cake. Shuell, who didn't particularly like sweet things, watched me with a smile.

"I'm looking forward to it, though. Your debut."

I looked up at the ceiling contemplatively, with my fork in my mouth. To be honest, the idea wasn't completely unwelcome. It wasn't as if I disliked dresses or accessories. They were annoying and uncomfortable, so I didn't want to wear them every day, but I quite liked dressing up once in a while. Come to think of it, I used to dress up and pretend to go to a ball when I was younger, but I hadn't had the opportunity to dress up for anything since then.

I was reminded of a young Shuell in a suit. Back then, he was such a cute little boy, all soft and fluffy, and the white coattails made him look like an adorable cloud.

Shuell was still pretty and lovely, but his physique was definitely anything but soft. *I wonder what he'd look like now wearing a suit...*

After several failed attempts at trying to imagine a grown-up Shuell in a suit, I finally opened my mouth.

"Yeah. Me too."

It wouldn't be all bad. Everyone I knew, except for Rietta, would be there. And I was curious to see Shuell all dressed up.

After I took my last bite of cake and washed it down with some water, Shuell tapped the back of my hand with his forefinger. Before I could even turn my head, a shadow drew over the side of my face. Shuell had leaned in, his lips by my ear.

"You'll save your first dance for me, right?"

I could feel his breath on me. "H-huh?" His question had been perfectly clear, but all I could do was stutter like an idiot.

He had backed off before I had noticed, and now tilted his head to the side as if confused at my reaction. It was then that I understood his words.

My first dance? Oh, right.

"Right. I guess I should..."

My rational mind immediately came to a conclusion, and I answered him without hesitation. I didn't have any suitors, and the only bachelor I knew was Shuell anyway.

Shuell beamed at me. "All right. You can't take it back, okay?"

His dazzling smile was totally pure and without hidden motives. As if he was genuinely happy at having secured his place as my partner for my first dance.

The next day, Derick convinced me to take some time off from work. We had a lot to prepare now that the harvest festival was right around the corner, and he said I should take the opportunity to take a break.

Derick was a prince of the neighboring kingdom of Archent, and he had met and married Marie when he had come here, to the kingdom of Maynard, to study. The former prince and current duke must be pretty influential, because when Derick went to work on my behalf, he immediately managed to get me some vacation time. Thanks to that, I was able to enjoy some unprecedented, extended time off from work, but my first day did not go very smoothly.

Was it on purpose?

The thought crossed my mind as I lay on my bed in the middle of the day, as you should when you're on vacation.

But still, why did he have to whisper in my ear like that? He could have just lowered his voice or talked to me later.

Ears are sensitive. When Shuell whispered to me, his breath had tickled my ear, and if I hadn't stopped myself, I would have let out a shriek.

There's no way someone as smart as Shuell wouldn't know that. I mean, it might be all in my head, of course...

Knock, knock.

"Are you in there, Wen?"

"Speak of the devil..."

It was as if he knew I had been thinking about him.

I was still in my pajamas, but they provided enough coverage, so I dusted myself off, stood up, and opened the door.

When the door did indeed reveal Shuell, I stared at him for a moment. He had always been handsome, but there was something different about him today. He was almost glowing, his skin reflecting the light like a shiny, freshly peeled boiled egg.

"Wen, you said you would save your first dance for me, right?"

"I did, yes."

"But you haven't been to many balls, and you've never danced in public before, so…" Shuell blurted out a barrage of words before I could ask anything. He bit down on his red, luscious lower lip. "Would you like to practice ballroom dance with me?" His apprehensive suggestion sounded cheery, as if to mask the tremble in his voice.

I was certain now. He was definitely doing this on purpose.

I took etiquette lessons when I was younger, and naturally, they had included lessons on ballroom dance. I was fairly hard-working, so my dance skills were outstanding. Shuell had taken those lessons with me, so he must have been well aware of this fact.

And he still wanted to practice? He was clearly making a move.

It didn't seem particularly calculated or sinister, though. The way he gripped the door handle, his fingers turning white, made it obvious that he knew what he was doing. He was clutching the handle so tightly that it looked as though it would snap off like a twig at any moment. There was something so clumsy and amateur about it. His ulterior motives were so plain to see that it made him look naive.

At the same time, it made me believe that his casual whispering last night couldn't have been on purpose, and I had to pause to think for a moment. He managed to act really smooth unintentionally sometimes. Like last night. It wasn't as though it had made my heart flutter, but he had managed to surprise me.

Since shock could also make the heart beat faster, it was easy to confuse the two.

As soon as that thought crossed my mind, I felt like running away. No matter what the context, the thought of being swayed in some way was not entirely welcome. But instead of rejecting him, I stepped back so Shuell could enter my room.

"All right. I think I've forgotten most of it."

I have to give him a chance. I had encouraged him to give it a try, after all.

CHAPTER
FORTY-TWO

It only took a few moments for our makeshift ballroom to be ready. It was just a matter of taking over an empty hall in the mansion, so it didn't take much effort.

In lieu of opulent chandeliers, we drew open the curtains to let in the afternoon light. Shuell was wearing a shirt, and I was in a comfortable dress. We bowed and curtsied to each other in a slightly awkward manner and stepped closer to each other. One hand on the partner's shoulder, the other hand clasped.

With a synchronized click of our heels, we took the first step together.

A slow spin, one step. Then another turn.

"Wen, it's the other way around."

"Oh."

Shuell gently spun me in the right direction when I tried to turn the other way. I followed his lead without resisting. It appeared that I had forgotten some ballroom dance steps, even though I was the star pupil of Madam Heidi when she taught us.

Next was holding both hands and taking one step back, then forward again, turning into his embrace, and then looking up at him...

I was focusing intently so as not to make another mistake, but I found myself slightly perplexed by Shuell's expression. He was smiling, but he looked uncomfortable somehow. As I was wondering if his clothes were too tight, I realized the floor underneath my feet was softer than usual.

No way.

I quickly moved my foot, and my heel made contact with the hard marble floor. *I knew it...*

"I'm sorry."

"No, it's all right. It didn't hurt." Shuell smiled as he told an obvious lie.

Though I didn't weigh as much as Shuell, I was still a fully grown woman. There was no way his foot didn't hurt after having my full weight on it. I let out a small sigh.

Outstanding dance skills? Yeah, right.

I began to wonder whether Shuell's suggestion to practice dancing hadn't just been a way to flirt with me after all. He might've been worried about his feet getting mercilessly stepped on at the ball. Maybe he had looked apprehensive because he had been worried about embarrassing me, not because he was flustered...

As I stood there, deep in thought, Shuell gently took my hand and raised it. He placed my hand on his shoulder and lightly held my waist.

When I looked up, he beamed at me. "Let's try again. I'm sure we can do it this time."

Shuell began to move again once I nodded. He led me with just enough force so that it wasn't at all uncomfortable. I relaxed and followed his movements, managing to take the right step, though it was off by a beat. We repeated the same move three or so more times, and once I managed to get the right rhythm, Shuell began to hum a familiar waltz.

The warm afternoon sun cast long shadows in the hall as our steps followed the beat, and instead of a grand orchestra, a pleasant humming filled my ears. We spun around, past the bright window, past the tapestries on the wall, past the clear line of sunlight and shadow bisecting the hall.

This is actually quite romantic.

I let out a chuckle at that thought. Now that I wasn't so on edge anymore, my body seemed to remember the steps, and I didn't turn in the wrong direction or step on Shuell's feet again. When I playfully leaned back and curved my spine, Shuell supported my lower back and twirled us around. Our eyes met, and we burst out laughing at the same time.

"I guess you weren't just making a move," I said impishly.

Shuell avoided my gaze. My eyes widened. Apparently, I was wrong.

"Maybe... I was. If you didn't actually need the practice, that is."

Hmm, I suppose that's true.

We were dancing close together, so in an ideal situation, my heart would have fluttered, but today didn't seem to be his lucky day. I was close enough to kiss him if I went on my tiptoes, but it didn't make my heart beat faster.

I smiled at Shuell, who looked a little crestfallen. *Your machinations might have failed, but that shouldn't make you sad.*

"Shu, if you hadn't encouraged me to try again, I would have left already. Then I would have practiced on my own until I was good enough, and only then would I have accepted your request to dance again."

Shuell said nothing.

"And I would never have seen how pretty the long shadows cast by the windows in the afternoon are, or seen the tapestries on these walls, or heard how beautiful the waltz I've only ever heard being played by an orchestra sounds when you hum it."

If I had left then, I wouldn't have witnessed this perfect scene, and even before that, I had been staring down at my feet, focused only on getting my steps right.

"You gave me the gift of a wonderful afternoon," I whispered.

So don't look so upset.

Because seeing Shuell look so downtrodden made my heart ache.

He chuckled. "You are most welcome, Lady Arwen."

"I mean it, my lord."

As we giggled and spun around once again, I suddenly smelled a scent that I hadn't noticed until then. I subconsciously followed the scent with my nose and lowered my head to where it was stronger.

"Did you use cologne?"

"Hmm?"

"It smells nice," I mumbled, taking another sniff. He smelled of fresh grass after it had rained, combined with freshly blooming spring flowers.

It suits him so well. Just as I was thinking this, Shuell spoke up.

"I didn't. Maybe it's the scented oil I used."

"Oh?"

It wasn't a ridiculous explanation; people did put on scented oils after they bathed. I still felt like it was a bit unfair. He wouldn't have taken a bath in the middle of the day, so it must have been a while since he last bathed. However, despite sweating from all the dancing, he still smelled of fresh grass—and flowers.

Maybe it's because he's the male protagonist.

Right. I didn't really think about it often, especially because he and the female character had become siblings, but Shuell was the male protagonist in the world of the novel we were living in. I supposed not getting dirty no matter how much he moved and smelling nice even though he didn't use any cologne was all part of the privilege that came with being the main character.

I took a deep breath to inhale the scent while I was at it. Although I did not like the humidity, I always went out for a walk in the gardens after it rained. I loved the fresh scent of grass and flowers. I took another deep breath, and Shuell froze. I bumped my nose into his chest and frowned, raising my head to face him.

"Stop... it." Shuell's face had gone completely red.

Oh.

I took a step back from him before I could stop myself. Both of our gazes wavered.

We stood facing each other, but couldn't meet each other's eyes. A tense silence filled the atmosphere.

He should have said something sooner. Was he just enduring it?

No, this is my fault...

The heavy atmosphere was suffocating. And at that moment, there was a knock on the door. It was barely audible, but I heard it. It seemed that we were close enough to the entrance hall, being on the same floor. Actually, it didn't matter whether I had heard correctly or not.

"I think someone's here. Let me go and check."

One of the household staff probably already opened the doors, but I quickly exited the hall. There was no denying that I was running away.

As I took long strides down the hallway, I put my hand against my cheek. The coolness of the back of my hand made contact with heated skin. I let out a long breath that might have been a sigh. My mind was all jumbled up.

My heart wasn't fluttering, but I was startled. So much so that the tips of my fingers had gone deathly pale.

It was too easy to confuse the two sensations.

He had said that he wanted to make a move. It might not have gone as Shuell had planned, but it hadn't been a complete failure, either. At the very least, I hadn't been completely unaffected. Otherwise, I wouldn't have run away.

"Oh..."

I let out a small sound and buried my face in my hands.

Meanwhile, Shuell was acting just like Arwen. He sagged onto the floor, his face beet red. He bit his bottom lip, glad that Arwen had left the hall.

He could clearly hear his heart beating wildly. The hall was quiet, so if Arwen had stayed longer, she would have heard it too.

She didn't seem to be aware of what she was doing, but she had pressed up closer to him as she tried to follow the scent. That was why she'd bumped her nose against his chest when he came to a halt. Shuell had been getting more and more flustered as Arwen pressed her body closer. He couldn't stop her, and he couldn't say anything because he couldn't move his mouth out of nervousness. All he'd done was continue to twirl with her.

And then, those two words were all he could muster.

It was an opportunity... I should have done something. I should've pretended I wasn't nervous. How nice would it have been if I just acted casually, like a mature adult.

If I didn't have the guts to do anything, I should have at least stayed still...

Left all alone in the hall, Shuell was dismayed.

I'm such an idiot.

It was another typical day of Shuell suffering from unrequited love.

CHAPTER
FORTY-THREE

Interestingly, and perhaps fortunately, the knock I heard wasn't my imagination. When I opened the door, a thick envelope lightly fluttered onto the floor like a falling leaf. It then straightened up and bowed like a human.

It was a sight that many might think strange, but I wasn't surprised. And at the same time, I realized why I had heard knocking on the front door.

Elvine, the kingdom's only sorcerer, often sent me letters with magic, and they would always knock on the door of the house. The sound was enchanted to be heard by me alone, so only I could hear when Elvine's letters arrived.

I took the envelope and headed straight to my room, my heart beating faster again from hurrying up the stairs. Then I picked up a letter opener and opened the envelope.

"Wen, I'm lonely all on my own."

The letter's opening remark was characteristic of Elvine's quiet, but odd personality. There was a faint smile on my lips as I continued to read her letter. The first two pages were mostly about how lonely she was and how her time at the palace was going.

"I miss you, Wen. Come visit me when you have time."

That was how she ended the letter. I took out some paper to write her a reply.

She seemed to be having such a hard time. I had anticipated as much, but I hadn't thought she would write after only a couple of days.

Thinking about Elvine sitting all alone in her Magic Department office high up in that tower didn't sit well with me. Elvine had been quiet and shy since we were at the Academy together. She kept her mouth shut tight in front of people she wasn't close to, and she lacked the social skills to easily befriend others. She didn't seem particularly interested in making friends either, so we didn't try to force her, but I still worried about her at times.

In the end, life was all about getting along with other people. The fact that Elvine had no social connections outside of her family besides me and Sia was probably not good.

Thinking about her made me sigh. We'd quarreled a few times because of this. It was a clash of opinions, to be exact. Sia was very outspoken, while Elvine was introverted. Having only us two as her friends, Elvine's attachment to us was bound to be great, and Sia was often frustrated by this. She would tell Elvine that she needed to make more friends, but to Elvine, this sounded more like advice given out of frustration rather than worry for her.

I could understand both how hard it was for Elvine to change her nature and how annoying her whining was to Sia, so I always tried to keep the peace. But that was tiring in its own way.

It would be good if Elvine changed.

It was important for Sia to use kinder language as well, but Elvine needed to change for her own good. I didn't have very many friends, either, so maybe I didn't have a leg to stand on, but...

I picked up a pen to write a reply to Elvine, but it was hard to think of how to begin. I wanted to tell her that I would visit her at the palace right away, but I didn't like going to the palace and having to deal with people staring at me.

"You should come visit the estate."

I crossed out the sentence I had written. For some reason, Elvine hated the duke's estate. Not just visiting it, but she didn't even like me mentioning anything about the place. Considering how introverted she was, Elvine had surprisingly clear likes and dislikes, and there was nothing she despised quite like the Severilous mansion.

She may be my friend, but she really is unique.

From the moment we met, Elvine had been an anomaly. Not only was she the daughter of Marquess Schreider—the role Rietta was supposed to have had—but there hadn't been any mention of magic in the novel in the first place.

There were actually a lot of things that were different from the novel besides Elvine. Shuell and Rietta hadn't gotten together, Shuell's parents hadn't died, and Rietta wasn't adopted by the Schreider family. And above all, the villain of the novel had died.

In the story, the main antagonist was Prince Deret, the brother of the king. He killed his brother, who had been a weak ruler, to take the throne before attempting to exterminate the Schreider family. Knowing that Prince Deret was a cruel man, I would have tried to find him and prevent him from doing anything the moment I realized I was in this novel, even if I couldn't stop him from killing a whole family. But when I looked up the royal family line, I was stunned. Unlike the other names written in ink mixed with gold, his name was written in red. It was how they marked deceased members of the royal family. Prince Deret had died from an illness at the age of five. He hadn't even become an adult, much less usurped the throne.

It was on the first day of my lessons that I'd found out this information. I was confused, unsure whether I should be celebrating because the original villain and future tyrant of the story had died, or whether I should mourn the death of a five-year-old boy. Prince Deret might have become a tyrant later in life if he were still alive, but at five years old, he must've been a child naive to the world. It was sad that someone so young had died, but this death was going to prevent the deaths of many others.

Marquess Schreider supported the monarchy, and the current king and crown prince were friendly with the Schreider family. Their bond grew stronger as Elvine started to work under the king as head of the Magic Department. Neither Elvine nor her magic powers had been mentioned at all in the novel, so it wasn't so odd that an unnamed disease suddenly emerged, leading to the boy's death.

After I decided what to do, I wrote that I would visit Elvine as soon as I had the time, sealed my letter in an envelope, and got to my feet. I was about to tug on the bell pull to call for a maid to ask her to send off the letter, but someone knocked on the door before I could.

"My lady, it's me, Emily."

"I was about to call you. Come in."

Emily entered the room at my bidding. She was quick on the uptake and immediately took the envelope I was holding. "Is this for Lady Elvine?"

"Yes. Please send it to the Schreider manor."

I hadn't written a name on the envelope, but Emily could tell who the letter was for. Sia didn't like sending letters, so the only person I wrote to was Elvine.

I smiled bitterly at my own lack of friends. At the Academy, I had at least a few acquaintances I would greet in the hallways, but I had been so busy lately that I'd lost contact with them.

Maybe I'll make some more friends once I make my debut.

"Oh, also, my lady..." Emily said as she put away the envelope.

I remembered that she had come to see me before I called for her, so I turned to look at her.

"Dinner is ready. Please come to the dining room."

I froze on the spot.

I took deep breaths as I stood in front of the dining room door. The staff guarding the door gave me a curious look, but I ignored it.

When Emily had told me that dinner was ready, I had wanted to say that I would skip it, even though I was hungry. Because Shuell would be there.

Naturally, I wasn't comfortable with the idea of facing

him right now. I didn't know how to face him, to be exact. The few hours that had passed hadn't been enough for me to gather myself.

But I couldn't skip dinner. Not only would the others be worried, but I couldn't just avoid Shuell.

Putting aside the possibility of dating Shuell, he was important to me no matter what. Even if I became sure that I needed to reject his feelings for me, I still didn't want to lose him as a friend.

Though it'll be a different matter if he then finds my presence hard to bear...

I took another slow, deep breath. I couldn't distance myself from him over something so small. Unless he started feeling uncomfortable first, I shouldn't make things awkward between us.

"Will you come in?"

"Yes. Thank you."

The dining room door opened, and Marie, seated at the head of the table, raised her eyebrows at me. "You're late, Wen."

"I'm sorry. I..."

"You ought to come immediately once dinner is ready. We were all waiting for you!" Derick started nagging me as soon as Marie had finished.

I avoided their gazes and quietly muttered, "But you always call for us too early. If we come here immediately, dinner is usually not even served yet..."

"That's because you never come downstairs on time!"

It was true. I hadn't just been late today. I would often meander and end up being late for dinner. I decided to keep my mouth shut and headed for my seat, the second on the right of Marie. Rietta's seat was between me and Marie. Derick sat on the left of Marie, and Shuell next to him. This meant that Shuell and I sat across from each other. Rietta and Shuell would often quarrel if seated across from each other, so this was now our usual seating arrangement.

Tonight, I moved toward Rietta's seat, because she was at the Academy. But that still meant that Shuell would be seated across from me, albeit diagonally. I forced myself to face him, meeting his eyes, and before I could greet him, he smiled warmly.

"Go ahead and sit. You must be hungry."

His attitude was the same as ever. I hadn't expected him to be so unaffected, so I found myself a bit flustered. Not knowing what to do with myself, I sat down, and dinner was served. Since everyone began to eat as if nothing had happened—which was true for everyone else except for Shuell—I picked up my fork. The food was as delicious as always, and dinner was peaceful with pleasant conversation throughout.

I was in the middle of enjoying my soup when Derick said, "Oh right, Wen. Madam Louise says she will visit in a week. Use that time to think about what kind of dress you would like."

My eyebrows rose. Madam Louise was a famous designer from the capital. She was as highbrow as she was famous, so not only was it hard to get an appointment with her, but she also rarely set foot outside of her boutique.

"Of course, she must come here. It's a request from the Severilous family," Marie commented firmly before I could say anything.

I smiled awkwardly. She seemed to have predicted what I was about to say, but it wasn't very helpful. Her remark made it sound like they were using their authority to boss people around. It might have been natural for Marie, who had grown up in this world, and I knew they were doing it for me, but...

"That's right. Please don't be overwhelmed. We may have made the request, but we didn't threaten Madam Louise and force her to come here," said Derick. He was trying to reassure me, apparently having seen my glum expression. But he didn't seem like he would back down, either.

I hesitated for a moment. Even though I had asked for their help myself, accepting their help and support without offering anything in return still felt like too much—all because of my frustrating mindset.

"Whether it's your dress or the date of the event, we will make sure your debutante ball is the best it can possibly be," Marie said, as I sullenly kept my mouth shut. "And Derick will be your chaperone."

At those words, I had to give in.

The other nobles had been weighing whether or not I was close to the Severilous family, and because of my career choice, they'd started to believe that I was no longer being sponsored by them. Derick and Marie would certainly be aware of the treatment I had received because of this—as though I were someone with nowhere to go.

It must have hurt them too.

"All right," I said, smiling. "Thank you."

CHAPTER
FORTY-FOUR

Fortunately, dinner ended in a pleasant manner. After we were done eating, Marie and Derick came and gave me a big warm hug. It had become an everyday ritual by then.

Marie held me tightly and asked in a low mutter, "Does it make you uncomfortable?"

Though I had been feeling daunted, her question made me chuckle. Despite her firm tone earlier, it seemed as though she was worried about me. I had known her for over ten years, so I knew she wasn't mad at me. Marie was very curt, but she tried her best. She spoke brusquely like a knight, but she intentionally made an effort to speak more warmly when talking to her family members, so she ended up with an odd combination of both. She didn't smile much, but she would often give sudden hugs.

They're good people.

I looked down at my empty plate as this thought suddenly occurred to me, but before I could get lost in my reverie, someone placed a hand on my shoulder.

"Wen?"

I slowly raised my head. Warm, pink eyes looked down at me quizzically.

"I thought you went upstairs already."

"I did. But on my way, I noticed that you didn't leave yet, so I came back." Shuell pulled out a chair to sit next to me. "Did you want to have some more? The sherbet was pretty good, wasn't it?"

Shuell looked completely unaffected, as if he really had simply been concerned about no one keeping me company as I ate more dessert. He seemed absolutely fine, which made my worries earlier about making him feel uncomfortable seem completely unnecessary.

"You..."

He might have really thought that I had wanted more sherbet, or maybe he could tell that I was being plagued by some feelings that couldn't exactly be identified. Either way, he was so considerate.

"You're all grown up," I said in a dazed mumble.

Shuell tilted his head to the side. He looked as good-natured as he did as a child, but any childlike features could no longer be found. He chuckled. "Did it take you this long to realize that?"

I continued to stare at his face, even at his teasing jab. His eyes crinkled into a smile. "You keep telling me that I'm all grown up. You've said that so many times."

"No, that's not what I meant..." I trailed off. I didn't really know how to best describe it.

How do I put this? Shuell seemed... experienced. He might not be perfect, but he wasn't as naive as I had thought. The Shuell I knew was kind and sweet, but inexperienced. He was full of love and knew how to share it with others, but he sometimes failed to do it correctly. I, of course, put up with it, but it would sometimes get a bit overwhelming. The worry that Shuell might be uncomfortable around me stemmed from that thought as well.

But Shuell had dealt with his emotions much more adeptly than I had expected him to. He was still being considerate and kind.

You really aren't the seven-year-old boy I used to know anymore. You really are all grown up.

"Kids grow up so fast," I muttered.

"It's been a year since I became an adult, Wen." Shuell pouted, looking despondent. His wide shoulders hunched over.

My eyebrows were furrowed as I smiled. "You're right. You're really an adult now."

I'd thought he was still a child I had to protect; a child much smaller than I was. I hadn't noticed he was catching up to me.

After that day, Shuell came to visit me every lazy afternoon. He always used dance practice as his excuse.

I smiled, seeing that this was an area where he was still a little inexperienced, but my smile didn't last long. Shuell was hard-working and didn't know how to take shortcuts, but he was also quite a lucky person. His strategy was always to stick with one thing, and whether that was by fate or by careful planning, it proved powerful.

Ballroom dance required us to be physically close, and because I hadn't practiced in such a long time, I still had room for improvement. So, whenever I did a misstep, Shuell would wrap his arm around my waist to steady me, and I would flail before reaching out to him on instinct. He must've been working out, or maybe he was born with it, but his shoulders and chest were fairly muscular...

Gah!

I shuddered at the memory that rushed to mind. Then I held my head in my hands in shame. I already felt bad for being consistently unclear in my attitude toward him, but now... *Fairly muscular? Really?*

This happened every time I got mixed up with Shuell. I had long since lost my composure. It was only natural. I might have been close to Shuell, and I might have touched him more freely than I would other men, but I had never put my hands on his chest before.

Unlike me, who had been startled, Shuell had been calm. His eyes had widened for a moment at first. But all he had done was steady me and say, "Focus, Wen."

I was dumbfounded. Since when did he become such a flirt?

I wasn't sure that this was the same man who had confessed his feelings to me day and night because he didn't know how to best approach the matter. He was the male main character, of course, but it seemed unfair for him to get so good at this in such a short time.

I let out a sigh and slumped over my desk.

The summer sun was warming up my room pleasantly. A summery breeze fluttered through the window I had cracked open. It was a perfect afternoon. But my mood wasn't great.

As I mentioned earlier, Shuell had been asking me to practice dancing every day. And after a week of daily practices, this was the first day that Shuell hadn't come knocking on my door.

Why?

The question popped into my head. Had he grown tired of it after only one week? How was he going to achieve anything without any perseverance? I breathed deeply at the sudden bout of anger rising up in me.

No, I shouldn't get angry about this.

It wasn't as though Shuell wasn't busy himself. And it wasn't as though we had promised to practice every day. There was always the possibility that he wouldn't show up, and yet I had relied on him to. I started to feel a bit unsettled. I had developed a Pavlovian response in just a week. Or I'd become the fox in *The Little Prince*.

With nothing to do, my head was filled with all kinds of thoughts. I recalled a famous line: "If you come at four in the afternoon, I'll begin to be happy by three."

Many people knew this line. But I actually preferred the paragraph a few pages before.

"But you have hair that is the color of gold. Think how wonderful that will be when you have tamed me! The grain, which is also golden, will bring me back the thought of you. And I shall love to listen to the wind in the wheat..."

I muttered the words as I wrote them down. My handwriting was crooked because I wasn't holding my pen very tightly. But it was still mine, so it looked as though I had come up with the words myself.

The grandfather clock chimed. It was three in the afternoon. Just like fate.

I looked down at the lines from *The Little Prince* for a while before crossing them out. There was no need to act so pitiful. I folded the paper in half and put it away before getting up.

I wanted to know what Shuell was so busy doing.

Knock, knock.

"Yes?"

When I knocked on Shuell's office door, I was met with a short response. It was one of his old habits to let in anybody who knocked on his door, regardless of who it was.

"Shuell, it's me," I said as I opened the door. Shuell, wearing a monocle, had been focusing on something when he raised his head in surprise.

I frowned. "Did your eyesight get worse?"

Even our butler, who was old enough to be a grandfather, didn't wear a monocle. Yet Shuell, who had just become an adult, was wearing one. Once eyesight deteriorated, it couldn't be restored. It wasn't as though there were things like Lasik surgery in this world.

When I took several quick steps toward him to check the lens, Shuell smiled briefly, touching his monocle. "No, I just wanted to try it on."

As I stepped closer, I could see his pink eye through the monocle, which showed no distortion.

"Why would you wear that if your eyes aren't bad?"

"Doesn't it make me look great?" he asked playfully.

"You're ridiculous." I looked down at the document he had been reading. Skimming through it, it seemed to be something about the family's finances. "Oh, is this something I mustn't look at?"

"There are no documents in this house that you are not allowed to look at, Wen." Shuell sounded uncharacteristically firm as he handed over the document, a list of items needed for the estate.

I exhaled as I read through the list. "Manufactured goods really do take up a lot of the budget, don't they?"

"It's inevitable, I suppose."

We sighed at the same time as if on cue. The Severilous territory mainly produced farmed goods and mined gems. The gems were then processed and sold, and because gemstones were expensive, the dukedom's finances were solid, and I had no intention of changing their stable source of income. And the manufactured goods I was talking about weren't simply things like ready-made clothes or furniture.

I envy the Schreider family.

I let out another sigh. In the kingdom of Maynard, where

business was booming, manufacturing was fairly cheap. Therefore, many guilds now sold handmade goods or products that could only be made by that guild, at much higher prices. Among them, the guild of the Schreider territory was the biggest in the kingdom. It created a wide range of extraordinary objects, and even my modern knowledge couldn't explain the mechanisms behind some of the items they sold.

It would be a different matter if those objects weren't particularly useful for everyday life, but that wasn't the case. The current number-one product was a lamp, similar to modern LED lights, that didn't require any fuel, lasted a long time, and didn't get hot. When I witnessed one of these lamps for the first time after being reborn into this world, I was sure magic existed here. I was astounded when I grew up and learned that these products were not a result of magic. After all, Elvine, the first sorcerer of the kingdom, had only made an appearance long after the lights had been invented.

This world certainly wasn't as technologically advanced as the modern world. *So how did they make those lights?* Perhaps there had been a big jump in technological advances limited to the Schreider territory. I had been so curious that I had grabbed Elvine one day and asked her about it, but she refused to share this secret.

The goods manufactured by the Schreider guild were

expensive, but they were also the most stable and safe. Because of this, just replacing the lights in the mansion cost a significant amount of money. The Severilous family was rich, of course, but I wondered whether there was a way to save some of that money.

I guess there's nothing we can do about it.

I put down the document and pulled myself together. When I handed the list back to Shuell, he put it away and looked at me for a moment.

"So, Wen, why are you here?"

CHAPTER
FORTY-FIVE

I was rendered speechless. I found it difficult to tell him the truth.

Because I expected you to ask me to practice dancing again today, but you didn't. It felt strange, like something was off, so I came to see you. I couldn't just tell him that.

Shuell tilted his head to the side when I didn't reply right away. Then a thought crossed my mind.

"I was wondering if Broschte could become a vassal of the Severilous dukedom." The thought had popped up suddenly, but I managed to convey it in a steady voice. It may have been a sudden thought in this moment, but it wasn't something I'd come up with on a whim. My family title probably wasn't of much use, but I had decided to stay here, after all. I had thought about it for quite some time, and it felt freeing to finally talk about it.

I was swept up in this unfamiliar feeling when Shuell smiled and said, "I see. That's great." His tone was even. He sounded happy, but not ecstatic or ready to jump up in joy. He tended to be surprisingly calm when he was glad about something. "I'll tell our parents. They'll be incredibly happy."

"All right. Oh, but I don't intend to become head of the house yet."

As the only remaining blood member of the Broschte family, I had enough authority as temporary head to deal with anything a head of house needed to do. It was a tiny territory to begin with, and there wasn't a fortune or many members of the household staff. Taking care of viscounty matters wasn't overly complicated.

More importantly, I didn't like the Broschtes. I was taking care of managerial duties for the few people who still lived in the territory, but if they decided to leave that desolate land at any point, I would have no qualms about never taking up the title of viscountess myself. It wouldn't be of much use, but I thought it might be good to transfer my authority to the duke and duchess and hand over the territory.

Shuell seemed to have understood my intention because he agreed without any further comment. Then he smiled, looking sheepish.

"I was wrong. How embarrassing."

"What?"

Shuell paused, then finally said, "I thought you came to see me because I didn't go to see you today."

I pressed my lips together tightly.

Shuell, not having seen my expression, continued. "I wondered whether I should let you know but decided not to say anything. It wasn't like we had arranged to meet, so I figured you wouldn't be waiting for me." He blushed. "But I'm still happy that you came to see me."

I gently bit down on my tongue.

You were right.

The response was practically on the tip of my tongue, but I kept my mouth shut.

I'd gotten used to spending my afternoons with him. He'd invaded my daily routine, and because he wasn't there, I was suddenly left with nothing to do. So, I'd gone to see him. But I couldn't bring myself to tell him this.

Because I don't love you.

I smiled—on the verge of tears. Still, he'd succeeded a little bit. He'd managed to rattle me.

I couldn't force my face to relax. We had just gotten started, but I already wanted to run away. Shuell had said that I thought too much, but that wasn't it. I was too scared.

It might have been premature to worry about this, but if I fell in love with him... would we be all right?

"Wen?" Shuell spoke up when I didn't respond. I slowly raised my head. The sunlight streamed through the office windows, bathing Shuell's golden hair in a warm glow.

The little prince left the planet without taming the fox.

When I'd read that book, I knew that the fox would forever be reminded of the prince whenever he looked at the wheat field, which was golden like the prince's hair.

Though Shuell had blond hair, it wasn't the color of wheat. It was more like the inside of a lemon peel or like sunlight permeating through a window. The hair that had been fluffy and knotted in his childhood because he had run around so much was now brushed neatly. But the color was the same.

I had been staring at Shuell's hair when I impulsively reached out. His tresses were soft against my fingers. His pure eyes, not unlike those of a puppy, sparkled like gemstones. I could see my reflection in those clear, pink-hued irises that were watching me.

I am not a fox, and you are not the little prince.

Like I said before, this wasn't really the time to be melancholic.

"Are you done thinking?" Shuell said. I wondered why he was letting me touch his hair. He seemed to have been waiting for me to get through my train of thought.

I beamed. Shuell seemed to have a special talent for bringing me back down to earth.

"Yes."

"What were you thinking about so deeply?" he asked, raising a hand to cover mine, then intertwining our fingers and lowering our hands.

His movement had been so smooth that it took me a moment of staring to comprehend that Shuell was holding my hand.

"Hey, you…"

"Yes, Wen?" Shuell smirked. *He knows what he's doing.*

It annoyed me, so I raised my fingers and dug my nails into his hand. He gently muttered, "Ow, ow, ow," even though my fingernails were not particularly sharp.

"Why ask? You seem to know already."

"I had an inkling, that's all."

Just as I knew Shuell well, he knew me well too. He knew all my anxieties and compulsions and the worries that stemmed from them.

Unlike my hand, which was gripping his tightly in an attempt to dig my fingernails into his skin, Shuell's hand was simply holding mine without any force. I could slip my hand out of his if I wanted.

"I like you, Wen."

The way he looked was familiar. The face, the tone, and those words. I knew where I had seen this before.

It was the last scene of my dream about him. Maybe it

was a prophetic one. I stopped gripping his hand but didn't pull away.

"That was great timing, wasn't it?" Shuell said, smiling innocently.

On that day, Shuell had told me that I thought too much. He was right, but not entirely. I was simply too scared. I was scared of the heartache Shuell would have to endure if he failed after investing so much in me. I was scared of him getting sick of my continuous worries, even if I did start to love him. And I was scared that if we dragged on this undefined relationship between us, we would end up drifting apart.

At that, Shuell had gently answered that we would be all right.

And, just like that, I was able to take another step forward.

"Ahem."

The sound of someone clearing their throat came from the doorway. I reflexively whipped my head around. The old man's gray eyes crinkled into a smile as they met mine. It was Sebastian, the head butler. Both his name and personality were perfect for a butler, and he was like a grandfather to Shuell, Rietta, and me. Because of his advanced age, he tended to leave most of the work to the other butlers or household staff and stuck to assisting the head of the family. So why was he here?

Just as I was about to ask, the warmth left my hand. When I looked back, Shuell was all tense and his face was completely red.

"W-why didn't you knock?"

"I did. Five whole times, with my old body. I took the liberty of entering because you did not respond, but…" He smiled broadly. "I guess I've interrupted you."

Shuell blushed even harder. His face was already as red as a tomato, but now it looked like he was about to explode. I watched dubiously as Shuell hid the tips of his fingers.

So, you do get embarrassed about things like this.

I had figured that he had become quite sly, seeing that he seemed unaffected by my hands on his chest, but the way he blushed at being caught holding hands was as pure as always.

Maybe he was fine as long as no one else was watching. I was considering what Shuell's standards for being embarrassed might be when Sebastian spoke again.

"It seems as though you should come and see this, Lord Shuell."

Shuell and I looked at him, puzzled. With Marie and Derick having traveled to the Severilous territory to inspect the area, Shuell was practically the head of the house at the moment. If his attention was needed, it meant that this was something big. Worried, I looked at Shuell. Had he been planning something without my knowledge?

"A messenger has arrived from the Archent kingdom. He says he has a royal letter from the king himself that he can't simply hand over to household staff."

Archent. A familiar name. Derick was from there.

Compared to Maynard, which was located in the southwestern part of the continent, Archent lay much farther north. Derick had come here for a term of study and met Marie, who had been in charge of introducing him to the kingdom she served, upon which they had fallen in love and married. Derick had seemingly cut all ties with Archent, as he never contacted anyone there, at least during the time I lived with them.

I was aware that Derick had been a prince of the Archent kingdom, but he had told me nothing more, so that was the extent of my knowledge. But it was unlikely that a sudden royal letter from a place that had never bothered to contact Derick was a good sign.

"I'll get changed and be there soon. Please ask him to wait a while," Shuell said, his tone heavy, seemingly echoing my own concerns. I patted his shoulder and left the room.

I hope it's not anything bad.

CHAPTER
FORTY-SIX

In the entrance hall of the mansion, I stood off to the side as I watched Shuell on one knee, all dressed in formal wear. In front of him was a messenger dressed in Archentian formal attire made of fur.

A royal messenger was regarded as highly as the king because he directly delivered messages from his monarch. That was why he didn't bow to Shuell, and why Shuell was being so courteous. Normally, this applied to receiving a letter from one's own king, but since it was addressed to a former prince of Archent and Shuell was representing him, it was a proper way to do it.

The messenger unfurled the parchment and began to read. Strangely enough, he started off with a date. "On the third of July, Year 873 of Morbisa, around four in the afternoon..."

It was now nearly two weeks after that date.

"...Ivan the Fourth, the owner of the Great Snowy Fields and the king of Archent, passed away."

The even voice of the messenger rang across the

entrance hall. My expression hardened. The late king, Ivan the Fourth, was Derick's father.

"The late king never forgot his son, who left the kingdom many years ago, and wrote in his will that he wished to see him again, so I, Morbisa the Third, command Prince Kendrick and his family to attend His Majesty's funeral."

The messenger shut his mouth after he finished reading the letter. Shuell seemed shocked for a moment, but soon agreed to the command and bowed. When he got up, Shuell's face was expressionless, hiding his emotions.

"Thank you for coming all this way. The Severilous family will treat you well for bringing us this important message. Please enjoy your stay."

At one look from Shuell, the butler approached. He led the messenger to a guest room, and Shuell stepped closer to me, looking troubled.

"I'm sorry, Wen." The apology came out of nowhere. I frowned, forgetting that I was intending to pat his shoulder in encouragement. Shuell gave me an embarrassed smile. "It looks like none of us will be able to attend your debutante ball."

Only then did I remember my debut. It hadn't even occurred to me due to the sudden news of Ivan the Fourth's death. But I continued to frown, and instead of patting his shoulder, I gave it a whack.

"That's not important right now."

"Of course, it is," Shuell mumbled, rubbing his shoulder.

And Derick raised this terrible excuse for a son so lovingly for twenty years.

I blew out a breath. "It doesn't matter. I'm just worried about Derick."

One of the things I'd learned from my two lifetimes was that family ties really were incredibly tough. My parents were cruel to me, from both a subjective and objective perspective. They didn't love me, and I knew it all too well. Still, if they'd ever changed, I believe I would've put aside the past and embraced them. As it turned out, they had been bad people until the end, and I had completely erased them from my heart now. But I knew how hard it was to do so.

Just as there were parents who loved their children no matter what, there were children who also loved their parents regardless of any abuse they may have endured. It was that way for me. As much as I was sick of them and disgusted by them, I could never completely despise my parents. I would get hopeful at the smallest sign of love. So, when they had said they would sell me to the count, it had made me sad. If they had been total strangers, I might have been angry, but certainly not sad. Despite it all, they were still my family.

Derick had not made contact with his kingdom for many years. He hadn't contacted his father, Ivan the Fourth, either. It was hard to say that they were close.

"Let's not worry about it now, Wen."

Shuell pulled me out of my thoughts once again. I met his eyes, which were smiling but clearly conflicted.

Right. He must have been worried too. If anything, he must have been more worried than I was—since he was Derick's son.

"All right." I pulled my lips into a smile and nodded.

That evening, Marie and Derick returned to the house. Unlike Shuell, who was acting like everything was normal, I couldn't look at Derick the same way I usually did when he greeted us with a cheerful expression. Shuell and I had agreed to relay the message to him after dinner, and just thinking about how he would react to the news of his father's death had me feeling uneasy.

I tried my best to act normally, but it was difficult. After dinner, Derick started a conversation with me, sounding worried as he dabbed at his mouth.

"Are you all right, Wen?"

"Pardon?"

"You seemed unwell during dinner. Did something happen?"

Yes, something did happen. It did, but…

I couldn't tell him that, so I made a long face. Someone then gently took my hand. It was Shuell. His warmth reached my hand, which had gotten icy cold. He tapped the back of my hand once.

"A royal letter arrived from Archent," he said.

Derick's face, which had been full of worry, changed as soon as he heard those words. He was suddenly frighteningly expressionless. It was hard to tell whether he was angry or afraid.

"When? Shuell, you should alert me right away when something like that—"

"The messenger arrived a few hours before you did. I thought it would be best to wait. Don't be angry, father."

At Shuell's soft words, Derick bit his bottom lip and took a deep breath.

"It was about the passing of Ivan the Fourth and a command for the Severilous family to attend the funeral." Shuell relayed the message quietly, as though it was nothing special. When he finished speaking, a heavy silence fell over the dining room.

I studied Derick's expression. He stared at the middle of the table without betraying his emotions, then hung his head slightly. Derick wasn't sad, nor was he furious. He didn't seem shaken by the sudden news of his father's passing, either. He looked completely blank, as though his mind was completely empty.

"Not a word while he was alive, and only upon his death…" His voice was as frail as a dying candle, but because the dining room was completely silent, with not a breath to be heard, he was perfectly audible. Derick's face was as gentle as ever when he raised his head. "I must send a reply saying that we will not be attending. I will not go to Archent."

I looked up at Derick in astonishment. He continued, his expression unshaken.

"It has been a long time since I left the kingdom and discarded my family name. So, there is no reason for us to go against our will. We cannot postpone your debut either, Wen." Derick smiled as he said this, as if he was completely fine. He seemed to have regained his composure, but all of us knew that he hadn't.

Though it was from another kingdom, it was still a royal letter, and Derick was still part of the royal family of that kingdom. He couldn't refuse to attend his father's funeral. Derick himself must have known this. He was not thinking straight.

Marie, who had been watching him in silence, said calmly, "Do as you wish, Derick." She got to her feet, then looked at my stricken expression and smiled gently.

"It's late. You two should go to your rooms and rest."

"Yes. See you tomorrow."

They said goodnight to us as they usually did. But unlike Marie, Derick still wasn't able to get to his feet.

They were putting on a calm front. They didn't want to look weak in front of me, or perhaps both of us.

In the end, I got up from my seat, unable to say anything. I smiled the way we always smiled at each other, said goodnight, and returned to my room.

The sun had long since set, and soon it was time to go to sleep. I changed into my nightgown and lay down on the bed—but couldn't fall asleep. After a while, I sat up to go for a walk. Putting on a thin shawl, I took a lantern with me and quietly slipped out of my bedroom. The hallway was quiet and dark so late at night, with only a few lights still on.

I slowly walked down the stairs and headed out into the gardens. As I followed the footpath, I could hear grasshoppers chirping. I headed toward one of the benches, but it was already occupied.

"Wen?" Derick called out before I could say anything. He was sitting on the bench with Marie. "Fancy meeting you here so late at night. What a coincidence. The night breeze is nice, isn't it?" he said gently.

He seemed to have recovered from his bewilderment back in the dining room and was back to normal. When I didn't speak, Derick got up and stepped closer to me.

"Why do you look so sad, my dear? Are you all right?" His hands, cold to the touch, caressed my cheek. When I still said nothing, he gave me a sad smile. "I apologize, Wen. I made you worry."

He seemed completely fine, apparently having completely regained his composure in such a short amount of time.

"Are you all right?" I asked before I could stop myself.

"Of course, I am."

In contrast to my voice, which was shaking, Derick's reply was cheerful. But his eyes, illuminated by the moonlight, still looked sad.

"My dear, you do not need to worry about me," he said, calmly meeting my gaze.

I couldn't bring myself to respond.

"I'm your father," the tremble in his voice steadily increased, yet his gaze remained firm. "I will always be all right. For you. Always."

It sounded like a promise to himself.

I felt as though I should ask him something. I reached out and held on to his sleeve, but Derick only smiled gently and removed my hand.

"Go back inside, Wen. It's cold at night."

It was the same as before. The mask Derick had put on, the mask that made him seem okay, began to crack.

I hesitated, but ended up turning away, unable to ask him anything.

CHAPTER
FORTY-SEVEN

I returned to my room feeling more unsure than I had when I left.

"*I'm your father.*"

"*I will always be all right. For you. Always.*"

What did he mean by that? It had sounded vague. As I thought about those words, someone knocked at my door.

"May I come in, Wen?"

Instead of replying, I stepped over to the door and opened it.

"Marie?"

Marie stood there, dressed similarly to me in a nightgown and shawl. Under the dim light, she looked strangely frail as she gave me a weak smile.

"Can I come in?"

"Yes, of course."

Marie nodded and entered my room, where a small light illuminated the darkness. She sat down on my bed and waved me over. When I sat down next to her, she took my hand.

"Were you shocked?"

"A little," I mumbled quietly.

I couldn't say that I wasn't. Marie patted the back of my hand but didn't say anything else. It felt as though she was signaling that she was ready to listen to whatever I had to say, so I spoke up.

"Does Derick not trust me?"

He had shown me no sign of weakness whatsoever. That wall he had put up was so tall and strong that I felt too intimidated to even knock on it.

Does he think that I can't be useful because I need to be taken care of?

The fact that it wasn't entirely untrue made my heart ache. It was true that I couldn't do anything for him. But I could have at least consoled him or listened to what he had to say.

"That is not true, Wen," Marie replied in a low voice. "Derick simply does not want you to worry about him."

I couldn't hide how hurt I felt. Her words stung. "Why not?" I'd taken a moment to compose myself, but my voice still sounded small and shaky.

Marie gave me a sad smile as I continued to look distraught. She quietly stroked my hair. "Because he is your father."

"But—"

Marie responded to my objection with a question. "Wen. Have we ever fought in front of any of you?" It didn't seem as though she was changing the subject, so I took a moment to think before answering.

"You always got along."

Marie shook her head. "You may not have been aware, but we fight too. Quite often, in fact. Over both big and trivial things."

I hadn't known, but now that I thought about it, it seemed obvious. Conflict was inevitable, no matter how much you loved each other.

"Derick did not want to show you that side of us. Though he knows he and I are not perfect, he thought he should be perfect in front of you," Marie continued quietly.

This was one of the first times I'd been able to hear about their inner thoughts. I listened with bated breath.

"He believes that is how parents must be, you see." Marie's profile, illuminated by the lantern, looked pained, and each word was marked with concern. "Derick refuses to show weakness in front of you. He rarely leans on me, either. He must always be a reliable father and a dependable husband."

"But that's..." I said before I could stop myself. Everyone had some loneliness inside them that only they could deal with. But that didn't mean you could manage without ever leaning on anyone else.

Unable to find the right words, I met Marie's gaze. She smiled knowingly as if she could tell what I wanted to say.

Marie and Derick always seemed so dependable and ready to provide guidance at any moment. They were certainly mature enough to support me and my lack of life experience. But both of them must have also been vulnerable and lacking in certain areas. I simply wasn't aware of them, just as I had been under the impression that the two of them never fought. I wished that I could console them, as they, Shuell, Rietta, and everyone at the mansion had consoled me when I was young.

"We all have things we cannot understand about each other. You do, but so do I. This is simply one of those things for Derick."

"Right. I understand." I felt I could understand, maybe just a little, why Marie and Derick had been so upset when I had told them I was only a temporary guest. "I would still like him to talk to me."

Of course, Marie and Derick had been upset by my attitude when I shut them out, but they had mostly been saddened by how much I had suffered on my own. Perhaps I wouldn't be able to understand what Derick was going through, but I still wanted to try. Because he was family, and I loved him dearly.

I couldn't stop worrying about him. I knew he was strong and mature, but still. I leaned my head against Marie's shoulder, and she lifted her arm and wrapped it around me.

"You should ask Derick once he feels better. If you ask, I am sure he will tell you."

I slowly closed my eyes at the calming rhythm of her patting my shoulder.

"Let us give him some time first."

A few days passed. Derick continued to act as if nothing had happened. But I could tell that he was avoiding us.

He joined us for meals every day and greeted us with a smile each time, but that was all the time he spent with us. He started to spend more and more time in his office. We all worried about him but didn't dare cross the line he had drawn. As Marie had said, we agreed that he needed some time to himself first.

After a few more days had passed, Derick called for me one afternoon. He offered me tea and dessert, and he was silent for a while, then finally managed to speak.

"It seems as though I must go to Archent."

It was what I had expected and entirely predictable. But Derick was unable to hide how bad he felt about it. He gave me a bitter smile.

"I am sorry, Wen."

I hurriedly shook my head. "No, don't apologize. This isn't something you can decline."

"That's true, but..." Derick grimaced. I felt as though I was reminding him of what had happened. I tried to put on a cheerful front.

"When will you be leaving?"

Derick couldn't smile, even at my upbeat voice. "In about a week. And it looks as though I will not be back for a month."

It was mid-July, and the harvest festival began on the first of August. It wasn't even close. There was no way he could be there.

"You'll find me another chaperone, right?" I asked brightly.

Derick, who had been watching me with a pained expression, nodded.

"And you'll get me the best possible dress and accessories, right?"

"Absolutely."

"Everything's fine, then."

"I'll do my best," I said to him cheerfully before pausing. There was something I had always wanted to say, but because I had never said it, it was harder than I thought. "Have a safe trip... father."

My voice was small. But Derick seemed to have heard me—because his eyes went wide. I smiled stiffly. "I'm sorry it took me so long to say it."

"No, not at all, Wen," Derick responded quickly. He seemed to want to say something, but instead, just bit his lip. His brown eyes sparkled, filled with tears, and he got up wordlessly and approached me. Then he enveloped me in a tight embrace and patted my back.

"Thank you, dear. Thank you so much." His voice betrayed his tears, making my eyes sting as well.

I never did anything for you, so why are you thanking me?

I raised my arms and hugged him back. We stood like that for a long time in each other's arms.

For the next week, the estate bustled with activity. Everyone was insanely busy preparing for both a trip to Archent and my debut.

During that time, both Derick and Marie, but especially Derick, spent a lot of energy preparing for my debutante ball. They were there to supervise everything—when the seamstress arrived and when the jeweler visited. Derick generally took on the tasks that were usually reserved for the lady of the house, and so it was he rather than Marie who was able to help in matters of high society. I knew all too well that he was doing all this in order to spread the news that the Severilous family was very fond of me, and while I was thankful for it, I couldn't help feeling bad about it, as I tended to do.

Everything went smoothly. The only thing I wasn't entirely happy with was my new chaperone. The person Derick had chosen to be my chaperone in his stead was Countess Elcanto. She was a noblewoman close to Derick, who had apparently always watched out for him ever since he had first come to the kingdom. She had a high standing in society due to her family's authority and her eloquence, and because she was so close to the Severilous family thanks to her ties with Derick, she was the perfect chaperone for me.

But for some reason, she made me feel uncomfortable. Her dark green eyes looking down at me were not entirely warm. However, she had never insulted me outright, and there was no time to look for another chaperone. More than anything, I didn't want to add yet another thing to Derick's to-do list.

Time passed by quickly, and suddenly it was the day the carriage left for Archent. Countess Elcanto and I stood by the gates to see them off. The countess had arrived at the estate two days before their departure, and during that time, everyone paid even more attention to me, as if they wanted her to notice.

"My dear," Derick said, "please tell the countess if anything happens, and do not try to handle it all on your own. All right?"

"All right. Please don't worry about me and travel safely."

Derick, who had been worried even then, finally got into the carriage. Marie's farewell was typical of her reserved nature. She simply gave me a tight hug.

Lastly, Shuell faced me, wearing an oddly concerned expression. I chuckled and pushed one finger against his furrowed eyebrows.

"Travel safe, Shuell."

His frown unraveled a bit at my lighthearted voice. He nodded and got into the carriage as well. The carriage did not waste any time and departed immediately.

I didn't even get to see Rietta because she left directly from the Academy.

The thought made me feel a little lonesome.

CHAPTER
FORTY-EIGHT

Once the carriage was out of sight, the countess glanced over at me.

"Let us go inside. It seems as though we have a lot to do." Her tone seemed to have changed. It was as if she no longer needed to keep up appearances now that everyone was gone. What did she mean by there being a lot to do? All the preparations had been made already.

The feeling that suddenly washed over me was too heavy to be described simply as fear. I tried to console myself. I tended to be incredibly sensitive when it came to communicating. The smallest frown or hint of frustration immediately rattled my composure. In my past life, and during my childhood here, I thought I had merely been sensitive to bad intentions. But having met many people who were nice to me as I grew up in this world, I had learned that those mannerisms weren't always a sign of malice. But the force of habit wasn't easy to break.

The countess had a standoffish demeanor to begin with. She insisted on using cold, formal language even with Derick, with whom she was close, and rarely ever smiled. It could be that this was how she always acted, so I shouldn't be so on edge.

"Yes, my lady," I answered. The countess turned and headed back inside the house. She didn't look back, but I followed her toward the dining room.

Now that I think about it, it's lunchtime. Maybe I should have insisted that they eat lunch before they leave.

As I was lost in my own thoughts, the countess entered the dining room. She sat down at the head of the table as if she belonged there and looked at me as though she expected me to sit down as well. Once I was seated to her right, the food was served, the same kind we always had.

As soon as all the food was on the table, the countess called over one of the maids she had brought with her. The countess muttered something in her ear, and the maid placed some food on my plate.

A piece of bread, some salad, and a bowl of soup.

"That is all you are to have," the countess said as the maid put the plate in front of me.

"Pardon?" I responded almost reflexively, and the countess frowned.

"You must watch your weight. With all that fat on you, it looks like you won't be able to fit into your dress."

I looked down at my plate again. *Oh.* I was familiar with this kind of diet. It was the same small portion that the viscountess had insisted on feeding me as a child, claiming that I needed to lose weight.

I thought for a moment. What the countess said was incorrect. The dress I was going to wear had been tailored to fit me perfectly, and my weight was completely normal. I had no reason to lose weight. Even if there was a reason for me to watch what I ate, it would be for health reasons, not for appearances' sake. A nutritious diet was key to losing weight in a healthy manner. This small portion made no sense. But it wasn't entirely incomprehensible when I looked at it from the countess' point of view.

Back when Derick and Marie got married, it was customary for the man to inherit the family title. Marie had managed to inherit her title after much ado, but she'd had to face a lot of criticism, and everyone had told her that her title would go to her husband as soon as she married. With Marie retaining her title and Derick becoming her husband but not the head of the house, more and more women were able to inherit their family titles, and things were very different today.

But the countess was a middle-aged woman, and her views were still aligned with those of the past. Back then, young ladies would starve themselves and wear corsets in order to look thinner. The countess was most likely under the impression that this was normal and correct.

But this could just be my being overly positive...

I decided to go along with it for now. I could always ask the cook to bring me more food later, and above all, nothing good would come from displeasing the person who would be introducing me to the other nobles at my debut.

I replied that I would do as she said and began to eat. She started on her meal once I did.

She didn't talk to me again during lunch. When I tried to strike up a conversation, she shot me a cold look as if I was being rude. I felt so uncomfortable, having become used to pleasant conversation during meals, that despite my small portion, I ended up suffering from indigestion.

The next day...

"Wake up, my lady." Someone shook me awake from my slumber. I blearily opened my eyes, having been fast asleep. "Hurry. You're late."

At the sound of the maid rushing me, I forced myself to sit up. I tended to sleep in, but I usually didn't have much trouble getting up when I needed to. Today, though, it was hard to shake off my sleepiness.

When I blinked a few times to clear my vision, I frowned as I noticed the sky outside my window. It was still dark. And when I looked over at the maid who had woken me, I discovered that it wasn't Emily, my personal maid, but the maid who had served me my meal yesterday at the countess' orders.

She had brought a bowl of water for me to wash my face and seemed to expect me to get ready. Having been woken up much earlier than I was used to for no reason, I was understandably annoyed.

"Is there a reason you woke me up so early?"

The maid was expressionless as she responded to my curt question. "The countess called for you."

"You mean to say that she ordered you to wake me up at this hour without even telling you why?"

"Even if the countess had not called for you, proper young ladies must get up and get dressed before the sun rises."

The maid was incredibly rude. So was the countess. She could have told me yesterday to meet her this early, but instead, she ordered her maid to wake and summon me without prior notice. I let out a frustrated sigh and brushed my fingers through my hair. I was becoming acutely aware of how much everyone at the mansion had respected my freedom. It seemed as though the countess saw me as being beneath her.

The maid, who had been watching me with an unwaveringly neutral expression, pulled the bowl of water closer. "The countess is waiting. Please hurry and get ready."

Do I really have to go? I took a moment to consider it.

I had to try to appease the countess as much as I could. But I had no intention of being dragged around by her like this.

Should I yield just this once, or go against her wishes?

"My lady?" I heard the hint of frustration in the maid's voice. I looked up at her without raising my head.

"Wait outside," I said calmly.

The maid's expression hardened. "I cannot."

"Then will you be helping me get dressed? You seem to have no intention of doing so."

Arguing was so draining. What I really wanted to do was lie down and keep sleeping. But I got out of bed, and the maid was forced to look up at me.

"I'm not comfortable with you serving me, either. I must insist on my personal maid who has always served me. Only she is able to meet my expectations." When I glanced over at the clock, I saw that it was only half past five in the morning. Only the servants in the kitchens, who had to receive ingredients being delivered, would be up at this hour. I smiled. "I couldn't possibly wake her this early, so I am forced to get ready on my own. So, wait outside."

At my quiet command, the maid looked at me with a frighteningly cold glare. But in the end, she bowed and left the room.

Once she had left, I let out a long exhale, and placed my hands in the water she had brought. I had expected her to be petty and bring me cold water, but it was pleasantly warm.

Narrow-minded people of the older generation, like the countess, tended to be very stubborn in their ways and would often interpret the objections of those younger than them as nothing but impudent defiance. Therefore, it was best for me to go along with her and slightly change directions instead of clashing with her head on.

After washing my face, I got dressed. When I came out of my room, I met the gazes of several members of the household staff who were already up and moving through the hallways. They, too, seemed to have been awakened earlier than usual by the countess' orders. When I gave them a sympathetic look, they smiled awkwardly, and bowed.

I followed the countess' maid, thinking about the many people she had inconvenienced. The maid came to a halt in front of one of the guest rooms and knocked on the door before opening it.

The countess was dressed impeccably, sitting there, and drinking a cup of tea. As I stepped in, she put down her teacup with a loud *"Clink!"*

"You're late."

The maid's voice had been cold, but the countess' voice was exceptionally icy. My hypersensitive instinct poked at my mind, but I simply smiled.

"I apologize, my lady. You didn't inform me ahead of time, so I arrived late."

CHAPTER
FORTY-NINE

I added a bit of charm to my apology. But the countess simply raised an eyebrow.

"I assumed that you would get up at this hour. Are you trying to boast about your laziness?"

"You must be an early riser, my lady. But here at the Severilous house, the day usually starts at eight in the morning." I tried to sound as uncritical as possible, but the countess' gaze did not soften.

"Your excuse is too long-winded. Is waking up late not a sign of laziness? Do not cloud the issue at hand." She clicked her tongue in frustration before giving me a look that told me to sit down. I let out an inconspicuous sigh as I did so.

"I've observed your etiquette and mannerisms over the past two days. They are disastrous," the countess continued without so much as offering me a cup of tea. I kept my mouth shut because I didn't want the tea anyway. It had been steeped for so long that it was nearly black. "We have scarcely more than a week until your debut, so time is of the essence."

This sudden critique of my mannerisms did not sound very promising. As soon as this thought occurred to me, the countess spoke again.

"Until the day of the ball, get up at five every morning and meet me here."

Oh god.

If I hadn't been so tense, I might have reacted out loud. Getting up at five in the morning? Even on days that I worked at the palace, I never got up before six.

"Yes, my lady."

Fine, I'll take this opportunity to become a more diligent person. I decided to think positively.

And I was actually a little relieved. The fact that she intended to teach me etiquette probably meant that the countess didn't despise me, though her methods may have been wrong.

"Thank you for taking the time to teach me." I gave her a small smile.

The countess, who had been watching me closely, got to her feet. "We must start immediately. Because of your tardiness, we wasted our limited time."

Sure, sure.

I didn't pay any heed to her unpleasant tone and got up as well.

The countess' lessons started off with me practicing walking with a thick book on my head without dropping it. I had done this as a child, so I wasn't bad at it, but the countess had something to criticize about every step I took. Telling me to tuck in my chin, straighten my back, be confident but elegant.

She wasn't satisfied with my gait the first time, so I had to keep walking until she told me to stop. This continued until noon, but the afternoon wasn't much better. Even during mealtimes and afternoon tea, the countess would continuously observe my every move. She said I held the spoon wrong, wasn't using the knife correctly, and that my shoulders were rounded when I drank my tea. Her loud voice felt as though it was echoing inside my head.

The countess' etiquette lessons stretched from early morning until the very end of teatime—a torment I've endured for three days now.

"Your posture, Arwen!" The sharp *clink* of her teacup hitting its saucer rang out along with the loud critique. I quickly fixed my posture, hiding how much she had startled me, but the countess continued to glare at me in dissatisfaction.

"You show no signs of improvement. You should already have mastered these things!" she berated me sharply. Her voice wasn't high-pitched, but her yelling was loud and weighty.

I kept my mouth shut and raised my teacup. My head was starting to hurt as I tried to pay attention to the correct angle of my elbow, the right way to hold my teacup, the direction of my gaze, and even the placement of my fingers on the hand that wasn't holding the cup.

"Lower your elbow. Raise your wrist."

But the countess continued to criticize me. I was so exhausted that I wanted to put down my teacup and leave the room, no matter what she had to say.

Is my etiquette really that terrible?

I may not have made my debut in high society, but I had worked at the palace where the royal family lived, along with countless other nobles. I was very much accustomed to acting according to noble etiquette. The countess was much older than me, and she had been part of high society for much longer, so perhaps that was why my manners weren't up to her standards. But I never thought I was terrible enough to be criticized so much.

"Never mind. That's all for today."

Luckily, the countess ended the lesson there. She let

out a frustrated huff, but I was just relieved to be allowed to leave. I got up, bowed my head toward her, and left the room. The countess watched me with her usual dissatisfied glare before turning away from me.

I dragged myself to my room and slumped down onto the bed. Before everyone had left, I had spent my afternoons practicing ballroom dancing with Shuell. I felt a bit lonely at the fact that no one would be knocking at my door.

As I sat there in a daze, staring at my quiet room, I shuddered. I got so accustomed to the countess' outraged yells that they seemed to echo in my ears. I opened the window. My room was too quiet. I needed some sort of noise.

As soon as I opened the window, the sound of the wind came rushing in. I exhaled slowly as I listened to it. Sharp words spoken in a sharp tone were triggering for me. I tended to freeze up whenever someone criticized me in such an intimidating manner.

A lot of time had passed, and I barely even remembered their faces, but I could still clearly recall the way they relentlessly berated me. I should have forgotten about it by now, but the memories persisted. Stubbornly.

To put it nicely, the countess was meticulous; to put it not so nicely, she was picky. She acted as though there was not a single thing about me that she was happy about. I wouldn't have cared if it was because I was truly lacking, but I was getting tired of her lessons. I wished she wouldn't yell so much. *No, I wish she wouldn't glare at me like that, at least.*

I put my head in my hands, agonizing over my situation. The window I had managed to open didn't seem to help at all. That contemptuous gaze, devoid of warmth. Looking down on me as if she was looking at something pathetic.

"I should go outside."

I cut off my train of thought that showed no sign of stopping. I needed a change of pace.

"So that's why you're visiting me so suddenly?"

"Mm-hm."

I gave a strained smile, avoiding Sia's sharp gaze. The gardens of Alfredo manor were full of blooming rose bushes. Looking at them made me feel better.

Thanks to my limited circle of friends, there weren't many places for me to go, so I headed straight to Sia's home. She was surprised to see me but didn't question the reason for my visit. Usually, I would never arrive without prior notice and preferred not to visit at all because I felt like I was imposing, so she must have thought something had happened when I showed up so unexpectedly.

She was right, and I eventually told her everything over tea and madeleines.

"Do you want me to leave?" I shot a wary glance at Sia, who was pouting. She must've been busy with her own things, and I began to worry a little as it occurred to me that I might be imposing.

Sia looked at me as if exasperated and pushed some cake toward me. She poured me a generous amount of tea as well. "Leave? Don't even think about it. Just eat!"

"All right, thank you."

So, she was just pouting a little. Instantly relieved, I carefully took a piece of the cake. The countess' lessons must have worked, because I noticed how hard I was trying to hold my arm properly.

The thick cream melted on my tongue, and I let out a small sigh. After so long without it, the taste of sugar was magnificent. Once the lessons with the countess had begun, I hadn't been able to eat comfortably at the mansion. I felt myself relax.

"How strange, though," Sia muttered, having been lost in thought for a moment.

I raised my cup of tea to my lips. "What is?"

"You said her name was Countess Elcanto, right?"

I nodded and took a sip of tea. It was delicious as well.

But Sia seemed determined to pull me out of my caffeine- and sugar-induced haze.

"No, really. It's a bit strange," she said solemnly.

"Why? Does she sound different?"

"She does."

I was surprised when Sia agreed with my joking remark.

"Countess Elcanto is famous for her warm and friendly personality. She used to work as the prince's tutor, and apparently, she never raised her voice even once."

"You can't compare me to the prince, Sia."

"Of course not. But the countess you described sounds like an entirely different person. There may be teachers who use fear and are strict with their students, but the countess has an entirely different way of teaching."

That different, huh? I raised my teacup to my lips again.

"Well, maybe my manners are so atrocious that the countess can't bear it."

"Are you serious, Wen?" Sia let out an exasperated huff.

"Of course, I am. I've never set foot in high society, and I only took care to watch my manners inside the palace. I never paid attention to my manners at the Severilous estate."

"As if." Sia's curt response pierced through my words and made them look like a weak excuse. I was rendered speechless.

"Wen," she continued firmly. "Your etiquette is flawless. Do you think I'm not aware of your perfectionist personality? You would rather die than show any sort of weakness."

"I'm not that—"

"Oh, yes you are. At least from my perspective. I've observed you for years, and sometimes you act as though you want to be perfect."

Her words stung. I put down my teacup.

"What the countess did was bizarre. She should have nothing to criticize about you, and even if you were so terrible, the way she acted toward you was discourteous."

When I found myself unable to respond, Sia blew out a breath.

"All right. Let's talk about this while we're at it. Why aren't you saying anything bad about the countess?"

"What do you mean?"

"You said she criticized you relentlessly for three days straight with not so much as a single compliment. Didn't that make you angry?"

"It's my fault she acted that way. The countess just expresses herself a bit badly. I'm sure she's not a bad person." Even as I said this, I felt my insides tighten. I believed it was true, but I felt uneasy anyway.

Sia watched me for a moment without a word before

she spoke again, sounding frustrated. "Does it make you feel good to believe that there is no such thing as a bad person?"

CHAPTER
FIFTY

I grimaced at her words. "What do you mean?"

"Exactly what I said. Does it make you feel good to believe that everyone has their reasons, no matter how terribly they treat you?"

"Sia." I cut her off frostily. Sia's tone was often cynical, whereas I tended to try my best to speak gently. But at that moment, my tone sounded very much like hers.

"I'm sorry," Sia said quickly, admitting her mistake. "That was too harsh."

There was a moment of silence.

"But still, Wen. You do that a lot. I know you're a good person, but that doesn't mean that you have to love and embrace everyone no matter what." Sia's tone had become a touch gentler, but it was still firm. I chewed on the inside of my cheek as she continued. "Just because you don't hate them doesn't guarantee that they will feel the same way."

I couldn't object to that. I felt embarrassed, as if she was uncovering a secret I had been desperately hiding.

"I know." I smiled bitterly. "You're right."

I know better than anybody that not everyone will love me, even without you telling me.

In my past life, there had been so many people who despised me when I was a child. They had hated me, even when I was far more innocent than I am now. If people disliked me back then, it's obvious some would hate me now.

"It's my fault for being so weak."

I didn't want to be hated, but that didn't mean that I wanted to be loved.

Some might say that it was enough for the people around you not to hate you. But for me, even malice from unspecified masses hurt me almost physically, and because of that, I found it difficult to badmouth anybody. I knew, of course, that I needed to defend myself at least a little and I tried to do so, but still, it was hard for me to show my dislike for someone. Any sort of ill will was so painful that I did not want even those I didn't like to dislike me. If I didn't oppose them and kept my head down, it wouldn't be as bad. After all, it was much easier to be understanding and believe that they all had their reasons than to admit that they simply hated me.

"Wen, please don't be like that," Sia said firmly. "If you dislike someone, go ahead and dislike them. You don't have to like them. Even if you aren't kind enough to love everyone you meet, those who love you will do so anyway."

It almost sounded like a command, and I knew that she was right.

"Don't waste your efforts on something so unimportant."

I know, Sia. But that's not easy for me.

I simply smiled instead of answering her. How nice would it have been if I could just change without much effort now that I'd managed to find the answer? Following through till the end was much harder and more exhausting than finding the right path.

I was doing my best, but whenever I was faced with aspects of my past, I would waver. I was still overwhelmed by the idea of being loved, was scared of being hated for no reason, and was envious of the people who loved me. I had used the fact that I hadn't been loved enough as a child as an excuse too many times for it to hold weight anymore, and I couldn't blame the people who loved me just because I had a hole in my heart that could never be filled.

The road to healing was so long and arduous that I kept wanting to give up.

How long did I have to live like this? What if I continued to be like this, even after a long time and after many attempts at changing? Would I ever be able to change? What if I had become twisted too long ago, from the beginning, so that I would never be able to change...?

I smiled bitterly once again. Shuell was right. *I think too much—way too much.*

"Don't worry. I don't just smile through everything without any worries."

"I know that."

Sia still looked uneasy, but I let her be and took a sip of tea. It had gone cold already. There were still a lot of sweets and pastries left on the table, but I got up without touching anything.

"It's late. I should go now. This was fun."

When I returned to the mansion, it was already past dinner-time. Thankful that I wouldn't have to endure the countess' criticism over dinner, I holed myself up in my room. I walked around in nervous circles before letting myself fall onto the bed.

Sia frowned when I got up first. Being shrewd and out-spoken, she figured out that I was avoiding the subject. I was well aware of the fact that this was one of Sia's strong points, but sometimes I resented it. Did she have to be that painfully blunt about it?

But still, I couldn't bring myself to dislike her. She had sighed resignedly but still escorted me to the gates. Then she took my hands and squeezed them tightly.

"Don't get hurt, Wen."

It was rare for Sia, who had remarkably high self-esteem and did not open her heart to others easily, to bear with all the trouble of caring about a person for extended periods of time. I knew what those words meant. She'd sounded both tired and concerned.

I flipped over and faced the ceiling. I was faced with the mural that Rietta, Shuell, and I had painted when we were young. It was obviously the work of children, but I hadn't painted over our artwork and had insisted on staying in this bedroom.

I was grateful to Sia. Though her methods might've been a little harsh, I could tell that she was worried about me and that she cared for me. Her words had hurt, but I was still thankful for them. Being very sensitive to ill will, I could tell quite quickly if someone bore none toward me. Even if their methods were wrong, I could tell who loved me. Similarly, I was vaguely aware of what the countess thought of me.

With a sigh, I got under the covers. I knew tomorrow was going to be a long day.

The next day, I woke up at five in the morning as usual and headed to the countess' reception room. She was, again, dressed impeccably when I entered. Before the countess ordered her to do anything, the maid approached me and handed me a few books to put on my head. I was about to start walking when the countess spoke up.

"Go and get dressed properly."

I was already dressed properly. I looked down at my outfit, trying to find fault with it, but didn't notice anything. When I lifted my head, the countess gave me a strange look as she said, "You must wear a corset."

I felt my features harden. Corsets were a terrible custom that had already been abandoned in Maynard. A physician had discovered that many young ladies sustained injuries from wearing their corsets too tightly in order to look slimmer, and now, no one in high society wore them anymore.

There was no way she didn't know this. No matter how you looked at it, this lesson wasn't for my sake.

"Do not tell me you cannot do it," she said with a derisive snort when I looked at her with my hardened expression. Her gaze was still full of malice. "You are not even a member of the Severilous family, and yet you are debuting under their name. Do you think what I demand of you is excessive?"

Her sharp words completely jumbled up my thought process. I finally concluded, took a moment to gather myself, and opened my mouth.

"My lady... do you hate me?" I asked her frankly.

The countess did not seem particularly surprised. She continued to look at me with cold eyes. "Judging by your bluntness, I see you still lack any semblance of class. I suppose that means three days of lessons were nowhere near enough." The countess raised her teacup as she gave her reply, acting as though there hadn't just been a moment of silence. She was still criticizing me. "Nevertheless, I intend to teach you up to the day of your debutante ball. You will never reach my standards, but you will be debuting under my dear friend's family name regardless, no?"

Though she spoke of her dear friend, her gaze got even sharper. It was unmistakable malice, so obvious now that I was amazed I'd ever convinced myself otherwise.

"If it is too hard for you, give up. It is as simple as that," she muttered languidly before putting down the teacup she hadn't sipped from.

The countess didn't answer my question directly, but I knew her answer.

Countess Elcanto hates me.

A lot.

FIFTY-ONE

"So, what will you do?" the countess asked when I did not respond. At the end of her sidelong gaze, the corset lay.

I had to decide whether to go along with her stubbornness or kick the door open and leave. Either way, the countess had nothing to lose. She had crossed a line, but she was technically only doing this to teach me, and since there were no other witnesses, all she had to do was keep her mouth shut and no one would know.

I looked at her for a while, neither reaching for the corset nor leaving the reception room.

"Why do you hate me?"

For a moment, the countess did not answer my question, which had nothing behind it but curiosity. Then she took a deep breath, muttered, "Why do I hate you?" and looked as though she was pondering. She had elegantly avoided answering my question earlier, but my repeated straightforwardness seemed to have changed her mind. "Because you are ruining this previously perfect family, of course."

And, as expected, I was met with a straight answer. I

listened to her without so much as a change in my expression.

"The Severilous family was flawless. Yet you continue to muddy the waters."

I was not particularly surprised. I had suspected that this would be her view of me from the way she continued to tell me that I lacked manners or was using the Severilous name when I wasn't even part of the family. But there was one thing I didn't quite understand.

"Is it because I am the daughter of a fallen noble house? Or because I wasn't adopted?" Rietta used to be a commoner, but the countess had not said a word about her. My intention in asking this wasn't to hurt Rietta. I was genuinely curious.

The countess gave me a derisive smirk. "Do you think you and that girl are the same?"

"We're similar at least. According to you, we both have a low status and are being supported by the Severilous family."

"No, that girl is different," she said in a firm voice.

Of course, we are. Rietta is much more lovable than I am. Apparently the countess had been swayed by her loveliness, and I was a thorn in her side in comparison. I wasn't jealous of Rietta. The fault lay with the countess, so there was no need to point a finger at Rietta.

Still, I did feel a little empty and disappointed. The countess, famous for being wise and benevolent, was discriminating against me simply because of my social status. It seemed that the label of being the daughter of a ruined household would follow me around forever.

If this was all, there was no point continuing this conversation. But the countess did so anyway.

"Rietta has already been of great use to the family. By adopting a commoner without discrimination and fulfilling noblesse oblige, the Severilous family has gained public trust. Since she is a girl, she can even help with strengthening alliances through a strategic marriage. But what about you?"

I stared at her, flabbergasted. I had not expected this to be her reasoning. The countess clicked her tongue impatiently.

"You are not a genius that could be of significant use to the family if they gave you the right education, and because your family was ruined, you have nothing to bring to the table. I thought you might at least assist the Severilous family by joining the household as a retainer after you graduated from the Academy, but you went straight to the palace to get a job!"

The countess was fuming with rage. She had never been kind to me once, but now she was pouring out her anger at me as if she had been holding back the whole time.

"You have not repaid them even a millionth of the kindness they have shown you, and you dare to lean on the

Severilous name to make your debut?"

I couldn't respond. It felt like I had been hit in the back of the head.

"On the one hand... at times, I feel that you are not at fault," the countess said, massaging her temples as though I was giving her a headache. Her eyes seemed tired. "But I simply cannot bring myself to like you. I suppose it is my shortcoming, for all I see are your flaws."

As Sia had said, perhaps she really was a nice person. She was benevolent to all but had taken on the role of a villain because she was worried about her friend.

"But I will not lend my aid in making your debut a success. I could not possibly disgrace the family name of my dear friend with my own hands."

She was only cruel to me.

I couldn't breathe. It was hard to face the countess, so I lowered my head. I had been so confident when I asked her why she hated me, but now I was trembling.

She was right. I was of no help to this family, to the people I loved. I knew that better than anyone. But despite that, the only reason I was still here was because of them.

Because they had asked me to stay.

Because they had told me I could stay.

I looked up again. Clenching my still trembling hands,

I met the countess' gaze. "Then why didn't you tell them?"

She furrowed her eyebrows at my defiant tone. "I did. Countless times. I told them to send you away because you were harming the family name. But since they would not listen, I had to take matters into my own hands."

Right. That's why I'm still here.

I inhaled before speaking again. "So, you must know that the reason I am here, and the reason I'm going to debut under the Severilous name, is because they wanted it." I could hear my own voice, but I couldn't tell what I sounded like, whether I was calm or ranting. "I understand you completely. But the person you should be complaining to isn't me, my lady."

She said nothing.

"It seems as though we won't need to continue these lessons any longer. I'll be on my way now." I got up from my seat and bowed to her, in the proper way, down to the position of my fingers that the countess had taught me.

Then I turned on my heel and left the reception room. I kept walking. I wasn't thinking about where I was going, but when I came back to my senses, I was in my room.

I sank to the floor.

Should I leave? I had finally started to feel better, but perhaps this isn't where I truly belong.

Various thoughts plagued my mind, as if someone was whispering them into my ear. I tried to clear my mind by recalling what I had said.

"So, *you must know that the reason I am here, and the reason I'm going to debut under the Severilous name, is because they wanted it.*"

"*I understand you completely. But the person you should be complaining to isn't me, my lady.*"

I repeated those words in my head and evened out my breathing. I was being overly emotional, and my anxiety had simply spiked because of it. My words had been correct. The countess had been displeased with me for not helping the Severilous dukedom in any way, and so she had tried to make me give up on my own by treating me cruelly.

I could understand her. But this wasn't my fault. We simply couldn't see eye to eye. Just because I could understand the reasoning behind someone's actions didn't mean that they were right. If I wasn't going to resent them because they had their own reasons, there was no reason to resent myself since I had done nothing wrong, either.

My wildly beating heart slowly started to settle down. I took a few deep breaths before staggering to my feet and sitting down at my desk. I clenched my trembling hands again and picked up a pen.

"Dear Derick and Marie. How are you? It's Wen."

After writing the first line, I let out a deep breath. I thought I was all right, but I really missed them. I was sure they would hug me, telling me I did nothing wrong, but I wanted to confirm it. Then, I thought I would be able to endure this situation. I felt somewhat pathetic for wanting to run to my guardians at my age just because something had happened.

But I never did it as a child, so it'll be fine if I do it just once as an adult.

I gripped my pen with renewed vigor but found myself unable to continue writing. The countess was an old friend of theirs. If they found out that she had been bullying me and that I had suffered as a consequence of their choices, they would most definitely be sad. Derick had said that I didn't need to worry about him, but there was no way that was true. Besides, they were on their way to a funeral.

After hesitating for a moment, I slowly wrote a letter to them. But it didn't contain any specifics; I just wrote about my everyday life. I hesitated once more before concluding the letter.

"I miss you. Please come home soon."

Before I had the chance to erase the last line, I quickly folded it in half and sealed it in an envelope. Then, with light steps, I hurried out of my room, unaware that I wouldn't be able to send the letter.

CHAPTER
FIFTY-TWO

Not long after, I had to dejectedly trudge back to my room, the letter still in my hand.

I had gone to see the butler to have my letter sent, intending to have it taken by one of the faster messengers. But the butler had shaken his head, looking apologetic.

"You cannot send any letters to them."

For a moment, I was struck by fear, thinking that the countess had given this order, but the butler explained before I could respond.

"Archent closes its borders during the state funeral. The duchess and duke are to arrive the day before the borders are closed, so even if we send a messenger now, he will not be able to get through."

It was an unavoidable reason. And at the same time, I felt anxious. I had been under the impression that I would be able to send them a letter at any time—but knowing that I wouldn't be able to contact them while they were gone completely shattered that sense of security.

I couldn't bring myself to rip up the letter, so I put it

away in a drawer.

Maybe I should go visit Sia.

I thought of this for a moment then immediately shook my head. She was already worried about me, and I didn't want to burden her any further by going to see her while my emotions were still all over the place.

I sat there in a daze. I felt like a child who was crying after realizing she'd lost her mother at a playground. *What am I so anxious about? Why do I keep relying on someone else?*

People grow stronger when they have people to protect, but they grow weaker when they rely on others. I was strong because I had to protect myself. Everyone in the world had their own problems, so I figured that it wasn't just me.

But seeing how weak I had become after hearing what Derick and Marie had said—that I was their daughter— seemed to have affected me more than I had thought. I had become vulnerable because I had people to lean on. But they couldn't always be there for me. I wondered whether this was a good change, seeing as I was having such a hard time with something that wouldn't have fazed me at all in the past.

I was trying to empty my mind, because agonizing over this wasn't going to change anything, but then I heard a faint sound at my window. It was like somebody was quietly tapping the glass. I stopped to listen, wondering whether I had misheard, but the same sound repeated.

I stepped over to the window. The envelope that had been standing upright and tapping on the window with one of its corners flopped down onto the windowsill as if nothing had happened. I let out a huff of laughter and opened the window. The envelope, which was light enough to have fluttered away just from the movement, stayed in place.

Usually, the letter would have knocked on the front doors, but perhaps Elvine knew what the countess was up to. This was the first time one of her letters had come directly to my window. *But how did she find out?* I wondered briefly before sitting down with the letter. I sliced open the envelope to reveal a one-page letter.

"Hello, Wen. I heard that the duchess and duke left for Archent. Do you want to come over to Schreider manor? You're always welcome, so don't bother to notify me ahead of time. You can come whenever you want to."

There was a reason it was only one page. The letter was short and to the point, but I was thankful for it. I didn't feel like being alone at the Severilous house anyway. Elvine had never invited me to her home before, so I was quite excited that I would get to see the Schreider manor.

I got up immediately.

"Wen!"

As soon as I got out of the carriage in front of the Schreider manor, soft gray locks appeared as someone came running into my arms.

"Elvine? Were you waiting for me?"

Elvine smiled and nuzzled into my embrace like a pleased cat. It was rare for Elvine, who was usually very quiet, to show such enthusiasm. *I guess she really missed me.* I stroked her hair as we walked into the grounds together.

A well-tended garden and a white mansion came into view. The Schreider manor was clean and arranged very simply. I quite liked this sort of design. But I could feel a stark difference between this place and the Severilous estate, which still bore signs of Shuell, Rietta, and me running around it in our childhood.

"It's very pretty."

Elvine stepped away from my arms, then took my hand. "I'll show you everything. We've got a lot of wonderful things."

"All right, calm down."

Elvine's gray eyes sparkled like a crackling fire. I patted her shoulder as I smiled. Elvine was very fond of her family and her home and would beam every time the subject of her family came up. It was only natural, I supposed.

In the novel, the Schreider family adopted Rietta. They had taken in a commoner, loved her, and raised her like their own daughter. Obviously, that meant that they must have done the same for Elvine. If she had been loved by her birth parents, Elvine wouldn't have been adopted by the Schreider family. I was glad that both she and Rietta had found happiness.

I let Elvine drag me around the place. She took me all around the manor and showed me all kinds of things. We passed a large library, a backyard full of herbs, and the kitchens, which smelled like freshly baked bread. The household staff we came across greeted us quietly but pleasantly, and it made me feel comfortable.

I took a few deep breaths, sitting on a bench in the gardens we had returned to. Moving around kept me from getting caught up in my thoughts, which was nice.

"I'm happy you're here, Wen," Elvine mumbled blissfully as she sat next to me with her head against my shoulder. I gave her a playful grin and tapped the tip of her nose.

"This is the first time you invited me here, you know."

"Usually, you're at the Severilous estate with those people." Her reply was accompanied by a pout. I had always been confused by Elvine's attitude toward the Severilous family.

"Do you hate them? Derick and Marie are good people. They would never have anything bad to say about you visiting me or me visiting you here." As far as I knew, Elvine had never even met them. It didn't make sense for her to dislike them so much.

But Elvine lowered her head without answering. It was clear that she didn't want to. I decided to stop asking.

"But how did you know I was coming? I never wrote back to tell you when I would be visiting."

"Magic," Elvine replied nonchalantly. *Magic?*

"I thought your magic controlled the elements. Can you see the future as well?" I instantly regretted asking about it so bluntly. She might have been ordered by the king to keep her mouth shut about the details of her magical abilities, and I was prying too much.

As expected, Elvine paused for a moment. But what she then said was not what I had expected. "It's not a secret or anything, but it's a bit hard to explain."

Hard to explain? Was there some sort of complicated math involved or something?

"Instead, I'll tell you about magic in general. How about that?" She sprang to her feet, her face flushed with excitement. Then she took my hand and pulled, wanting me to get up. I stayed seated as I looked up at her.

"Did something happen to you today?"

Elvine tilted her head to the side in confusion. "Why do you ask?"

"You're acting a little..."

...strange today.

I closed my mouth, thinking that my intended words might sound a bit too blunt. Nevertheless, her behavior was really strange. Elvine was definitely acting differently today. Her clear enthusiasm couldn't solely be attributed to her excitement to see me. Sure, I had never asked to be invited to the Schreider manor myself, so maybe my visit was reasonably exciting, but Elvine had always kept her mouth shut when it came to magic.

"Is it really alright for you to tell me about magic?"

"Of course. It's you, after all." Her reply was effortless, but I was still concerned. I had a strong feeling that what Elvine was about to tell me about magic would be very different from what was widely known. I didn't want to overhear some sort of state secret. It could make things difficult for me.

"But it's been kept secret for so long."

Elvine nodded at my worried voice. I felt a bit betrayed

at the way she didn't hesitate to dismiss my concerns. "It's nothing special. It's just the origin and principles of magic. You won't be held responsible by anyone for hearing about this," Elvine added before I could tell her I didn't want to hear it. She spoke quickly, but her eyes were glinting again.

I let out a sigh and got to my feet.

CHAPTER
FIFTY-THREE

Elvine took me to a small room, slightly smaller than my own bedroom and furnished with the same kind of sleek furniture as the rest of the house.

I looked around the room. "Elvine?" I said apologetically.

"Hmm?"

"I don't think I can sleep over tonight..."

Elvine looked surprised. "I know. You didn't say you would."

"Then why did you bring me to a guest room?"

The room was luxurious enough, but that was it. It had no personality, and it only included bare necessities. I frowned slightly as my eyes spotted a layer of dust on the chest of drawers, and the unmade bed. Even if this wasn't the nicest guest room, it was still odd for it to be in such a state of disarray. This was a clear oversight by the household staff who were getting paid to clean the place.

I sighed inwardly, unable to criticize the goings-on in someone else's house, but then Elvine said, "This is my room, Wen."

It took me a moment to process her casual words. I thought I had heard wrong. "It's your room?"

"Yes. It used to be a guest room. About... thirteen years ago," Elvine replied, her eyebrows drawn together as she tried to remember the details.

That was around the time Elvine got adopted.

"When I first arrived here, my mother gave me this room. But later she said it would be a bother to redecorate a different room and asked if I could just stay here, so I did."

Something felt odd about her answer. Even in my eyes—and I had no eye for decoration—this room was clearly not as nice as the others. Even if Elvine had wanted to stay here, with the amount of money the Schreider family had, decorating it would have been no problem.

As I stood there in a daze, Elvine walked over to the couch and patted the seat next to her, gesturing for me to sit down. I put on a smile over my uneasy expression and stepped closer to her. Elvine had been notorious for trashing her room—even back at the Academy. She didn't care whether her room looked like a pigsty, so I supposed that it would be fine if she was happy with this room.

"Elvine."

"Hmm?"

"There's a maid at our house who is great at cleaning. I'll

write a letter of recommendation. Would you hire her here?"

Elvine was always happy whenever Sia and I cleaned up her room, so it no longer looked like an explosion had gone off in it. Dust wasn't good for you anyway, and I thought I might feel better if this room was at least cleaned properly. Elvine beamed and nodded.

I let out a huff of laughter. "So, you hate everyone else at the Severilous estate, but you're fine with a maid who works there?"

At my teasing, Elvine's expression grew stiff. She seemed to be thinking over her words before looking up, apparently having made a decision. "Well, it's someone you're recommending."

"I'm from the Severilous house too, though."

Her face had softened for a moment but hardened again at my words. She looked like a cat whose toy had been taken away, which made me laugh. Elvine grumbled as she got to her feet, but then she wordlessly wrapped her arms around me.

"Can't you just live here?"

I knew her words were nothing but thoughtless whining, but they shook me. I smiled sadly and raised my arms to hug Elvine back. The Severilous mansion had become uncomfortable for me in a matter of days. To be honest, right now, it felt like this place might be more pleasant to stay in. But everyone would be returning soon enough, and the countess wasn't going to stay at the mansion forever.

"I can't. This is not my home."

"But it could be your home, right?" Elvine looked at me with puppy-dog eyes.

I poked her forehead lightly and changed the subject. "You said you would tell me about magic. Don't keep me waiting any longer."

Fortunately, Elvine let me distract her. She clapped her hands together as if she had forgotten about her promise to tell me about magic and led me back to the couch.

"First of all, magic comes from nature."

"Right, I know that much. Water, fire, wind—stuff like that, right?"

"No, it's much more fundamental and extensive than that." Elvine shook her head and took a moment to think before snapping her fingers. A small flame flickered to life on her fingertip. "Like I said, it looks a lot like fire, water, and wind, but... it's more accurate to say that the basic element gets dressed up to appear like that. And if you gather more energy, you can make it much bigger and wield greater power."

Elvine's voice was quiet as she explained, and I listened with rapt attention. I thought magic was tied to elementals, like in the fantasy novels from my past life, but this didn't necessarily seem to be the case.

"That basic element is called mana, and a sorcerer's power depends on how much mana they can wield."

"I see." A sudden question came to mind as I listened. Her explanation was quite systematic. "Did you lay all this out after finding out about it yourself? Because there might be more sorcerers in the future?"

Elvine was quiet for a moment, but then shook her head. "No, it was all recorded by the Schreider family."

All of this about sorcerers? I frowned. Elvine was the kingdom's only sorcerer. So how were there records about others?

"A long time ago, there were many sorcerers on the continent. They didn't make up the majority of the population, but there was more than one, at least. These records were all written by them. The Schreider family preserved them and handed them over to me because I am a sorcerer."

Elvine told me this very calmly, but it was shocking. *There used to be other sorcerers?* None of that had ever been mentioned in the kingdom's history.

"But why are you the only one now?"

Elvine's expression darkened. She mumbled dejectedly, "They were all killed because they were seen as demons for having powers that other humans didn't, you see."

"But they could use magic, right? And those opposing them couldn't."

I wondered how they could have all been killed, even if they had been outnumbered. Did they have no chance to negotiate?

"I told you that a sorcerer's power depends on how much mana they can wield, right?" Elvine said, having apparently sensed my confusion. "The ability to wield mana is partly genetic but also has a lot to do with practice. The sorcerers all attempted to use large amounts of mana at once because their lives were threatened, which caused the mana to disperse altogether. If they had all gathered together and let the strongest among them wield all of the mana, they would've all survived. But the severe persecution they faced didn't allow them that chance. In the end, the sorcerers couldn't even fight back before they were massacred. Their books were burned, and their very existence was erased from history."

I found myself unable to respond as I listened to Elvine. Her expression had darkened significantly and was showing grief, fury, and remorse.

"And after a long, long time, another sorcerer was born. Me."

A sorcerer was different from other people. They could

even be called a different species altogether. And Elvine was all alone in this world, with no one else like her.

It made me feel sorry for her, but at the same time, I felt a distance between us. I didn't let it show, however, and patted the back of her hand. "They're at peace now."

One person struggling to do what was best for the many had to be difficult. I didn't want Elvine to dedicate herself to avenging her people who were killed a long time ago.

Fortunately, Elvine's face soon brightened. "I'm all right. I have my own family now."

Good. If you're all right, that's enough. I wanted to stop thinking about the matter with that conclusion, but Elvine continued.

"Oh, right. So the way magic manifests itself..." She seemed to have cheered up again because her eyes were sparkling again. "I can see things," she exclaimed gleefully. Her tone was bright, but something was off. But before I could dwell on it, she kept talking. "There are round ones, spiky ones, and ones with sharp angles. They kind of hover around me and scream in my ears."

"What?" I froze. Her carefree tone didn't at all suit what she was telling me. It struck me as bizarre.

Elvine seemed confused by my reaction, but she continued. "I have no idea what they're saying. But when I ask them internally to do something for me, they do. I think they might be aggregates of mana." Elvine turned to stare at me expectantly.

Unable to respond, I stared back at her in awe. That unsettling feeling I had tried to ignore came over me all at once. I hesitated for a moment before finally managing to say something.

"Are you all right?"

I returned to the Severilous house before dinnertime. Though I had left that morning in a great mood, I felt completely exhausted now. Sitting on a chair, I recalled the conversation I'd had with Elvine.

When I'd asked her whether she was all right, Elvine gave me another confused look. For someone who had just shared that she could see bizarre things that were screaming in her ear incessantly, she looked unreasonably calm. It made me feel like I was the strange one, so I paused for a moment before speaking again.

"I can't possibly imagine. If there were things only I could see and hear, I..." I took a moment to think of the best way to say it. How did I convey my worries without hurting Elvine? "Doesn't it bother you?"

"Hmm?" Elvine tilted her head to the side casually at the words I managed to finally blurt out. She pouted briefly, but then her expression quickly returned to normal. "It is a little annoying. But they're the reason I can use magic. I'm happy that my magic allows me to help with a lot of things." She had smiled at that, and her smile had been as pure as ever. It really seemed as though she was simply happy to be able to help people.

Elvine had always been like that. She rarely complained and always seemed pleased to help whenever we asked her. She was a kind and good friend. That hadn't changed, but for some reason, she'd acted awkwardly today. No, the entire Schreider family had.

How do they have records of sorcerers?

Sorcerers never came up in any history lessons at the Academy. They might have come up in the context of slaying monsters, but they must have been persecuted severely if there was no trace of them in the history books. The kingdom was huge, and there were plenty of people who might still have owned a few records about the sorcerers, but why the Schreider family?

I quickly shook my head. They could've procured them because their newly adopted daughter happened to be a sorcerer. And since the king was fond of Elvine, they may have gotten permission to access tomes forbidden to others in order to help her.

It made perfect sense and was completely reasonable.

But then why did I feel so anxious about it?

It felt as though I was missing something. I couldn't

quite put my finger on it, but something felt off. The origin and use of magic. The history of sorcerers and Elvine. The Schreider family members, none of whom seemed to be present, and Elvine's dusty drawers.

Is it all connected?

I was lost in thought when I heard someone knock at my door.

"My lady. It's Emily."

What does she want?

When I told her to come in, Emily entered the room with a trolley. "You weren't able to eat dinner. I brought you some food."

As Emily uncovered the dish, the smell of something delicious wafted over to me—beef stew and freshly baked bread. My mouth began to water, and my stomach growled. The sun had already gone down, and I hadn't even had lunch. I looked longingly at the delicious food before turning to Emily.

"Is it all right for you to bring me all this, though? The countess might get angry."

There wasn't much she could do to me besides scold me, but Emily, as a member of the household staff, could receive punishment. Derick and Marie had entrusted the countess with me, and as long as they were gone, she was in control of the house.

At my worried tone, Emily's face instantly turned devilish. I was taken aback at how suddenly her serenely smiling face switched.

"I don't care if that old witch gets mad—"

"Emily!" I exclaimed in complete shock.

Emily grinned as if she didn't say anything, but I had heard what she muttered loud and clear.

"Did Rietta rub off on you? How could you say that!"

If what Emily had just said somehow got out, she wouldn't be able to get away with it. In a world ruled by a class system, the thought of a commoner insulting a noble was unthinkable.

"There is no such thing as a well-kept secret. What if someone overheard you and reported it to the countess?"

Only when I scolded her did Emily lose her grin. "But, my lady," she mumbled, "all the other maids say it too. Besides, this is your room, and I said it quietly. No one could have overheard."

"Still! You never know. Don't even think about saying something like that again!"

People might think I was overreacting, but there was no helping it. A zero percent chance was still better than a one-thousandth percent chance. Emily was very dear to me, and I didn't want to lose her.

Emily watched me warily. "But, my lady," she said, sounding hurt. "Isn't it frustrating?"

I was rendered speechless. I couldn't deny it.

"Everyone at the estate knows the countess is going too far. We may be serving her for now, but we are part of the Severilous household." Emily bit down on her lip as if in anger. Her brown eyes glinted dangerously. "Even the duchess herself doesn't scold you, and yet the countess dares..." She ground her teeth in frustration before looking at me with a sympathetic gaze.

"My lady, please don't hold back if you're angry. You should at least yell and throw some vases. We'll take care of the cleanup, all right?"

"What are you talking about, Emily? I couldn't do that even if I was angry," I responded firmly.

What is she saying?

"But the other young noble ladies all act like that when they're angry."

"That may be true, but that's not how Rietta and I act, right?"

Even as I said so, I felt a bit uneasy. Emily had been working for the Severilous household ever since I came to live here. I knew that rumors spread quickly among maids, so she could have heard it from maids serving at a different house, but I wondered whether Rietta had ever been that vicious.

I recalled the last time Rietta had been angry. It had been... a few months ago now. When she had a big fight with Shuell. Back then, Rietta had ripped up Shuell's pillow, kicked some trees, and run through the hallways of the mansion, screaming.

Hmm. I should make Rietta transcribe some law books when she returns. She really needed to work on that temper of hers.

Having finished my train of thought, I sat down and lifted a spoon. When my stomach growled once more, Emily, who had been pouting in silence, seemed alarmed.

"Oh my, I'm so sorry to keep you waiting. Please go ahead, my lady. You must be hungry. The cook tried hard to make the stew particularly delicious for you today. And he made bread from scratch as well."

"Thank you. It looks amazing."

I took a spoonful of stew. It tasted familiar, just like the stew I had eaten growing up. It wasn't anything new, which made it more comforting.

"Once you're done with your dinner, let's try on your dress. While you were at the Schreider manor, Madam sent over the finished dress. We'll do your hair again and pick out which accessories will go best with it." Emily continued to chatter as I ate, trying her best to entertain me.

I must have made her worry. *I feel fine, though.* I smiled bitterly and let Emily drag me around to her heart's content.

Since the day I'd said I would no longer need any lessons and stormed out of the reception room, the countess had not messed with me at all. Though we were staying in the same building, we never ran into each other. While we ignored each other, the household staff took extra care of me as if I was a toddler, so it was actually much nicer now than it had been.

Time passed, and the day of my debut finally arrived.

In my past life, the harvest festival took place in November, after all the harvesting had been done. But in Maynard, the harvest festival was held in August, just before the actual harvesting. The kingdom had no doubt that the harvest would be plentiful, and so the festival was held in anticipation of this. This was possible because the kingdom, with its rich soil and pleasant weather, had never experienced a bad harvest. The farmers would be exhausted once it was over, so the period afterward was designated for rest. The festival was meant to help the farmers build up their energy, and also to use up all the produce from the previous year to make room for this year's harvest.

Because of this, all of Maynard smelled of freshly baked bread on the first day of the harvest festival. It was tradition among commoners to share bread baked in the traditional way, and the nobles did their part by baking bread and giving it to the poor.

The harvest festival, which took place over four short but full days, was a joyous and tumultuous occasion for both commoners and nobles. Though I had been too busy with work at the palace during the harvest festivals in the last two years, this year was different.

"My lady, it is time to leave."

I had been sitting by the window, taking in the scent of freshly baked bread, when I heard Emily's call and got out of my chair. I looked down at my hands, clad in white satin gloves. The green chiffon dress I was wearing fluttered around me like fairy wings whenever I moved. I slowly went down the stairs and headed toward the entrance hall.

Waiting for me, in an elegant green dress, was the countess.

CHAPTER
FIFTY-FIVE

I couldn't stop my eyes from going wide. The countess predictably furrowed her eyebrows at my reaction. I quickly schooled my features, but I was still in shock. The countess clicked her tongue at me before turning away.

"Let us go."

I followed the countess as she walked toward the carriage with the Severilous family crest parked outside the front doors. She got into the carriage and gave me an expectant look, so I followed her inside. Once we were seated, the carriage began to move slowly. Despite wearing an uncomfortable dress, I felt comfortable in my seat. The carriage was high-end and was extremely comfortable to ride.

I tried not to show how surprised I was as I sank into my thoughts.

Why is she here?

I had figured that there was no chance the countess would be my chaperone after the moment I said I no longer needed lessons. She had already been so displeased with me before that point that it made no sense to expect it. I thought she would make some sort of excuse, saying that she felt unwell, and use that as a reason to avoid the ball.

Whether or not a young noble lady made her debut with a chaperone made a substantial difference. Because it would be her first foray into high society, the chaperone's connections would become hers. Which meant that young ladies without a chaperone would be hard-pressed to make any connections at all. Derick and Marie would, of course, take care of me once they were back, but messing up my debut was an entirely different matter. I had prepared myself for it but was still worried.

Did she change her mind?

I was in the middle of deliberating all of this when the carriage came to a halt. The ball was being held at the biggest banquet hall in the royal palace. I took care not to step on my dress, something I hadn't worn in a while, as I made my way toward the hall.

"Countess Elcanto and the daughter of Viscount Broschte!" The loud voice of the attendant announcing our arrival rang across the hall and had people turning their gazes toward us.

I couldn't get used to the sight of people covering their mouths with fans or their hands and whispering. I kept my back straight and my head held high as I approached the king sitting on the throne.

"Henrietta of Elcanto greets His Glorious Majesty."

So, her name is Henrietta, I pondered idly as I bowed my head toward the king. When I raised my head again at his command, he gave me a warm smile. The crown prince standing next to him wore the same expression. According to the novel, both of them should have been dead by now, so it did feel a bit peculiar to see them alive and well. But it wasn't a bad feeling.

Once we stepped away from the king after greeting him, most of the focus on us had dissipated, but there were still a few pointed gazes directed at me. They seemed to be waiting for the countess to introduce me. I was starting to get nervous, and I took a few deep breaths when the countess suddenly muttered something.

"My dress is uncomfortable. They must have failed to take out all the pins." Her brow was creased, and she looked genuinely bothered. "I will go to the powder room. Wait for me here."

I agreed to do so, and she left the banquet hall. My eyes followed her for a moment before I turned away. There were a few familiar faces, but they were all already engaged in their own conversations. I wasn't particularly close to any of them, so I didn't bother to approach anyone. It was better to wait for the countess to introduce me so as not to earn any disapproval.

Though this was the day of my debut, the Severilous household staff had made sure I didn't starve. Thanks to the decent meal I had, I wasn't too stuffed or hungry. I picked up a glass of lime juice from a passing waiter before heading to a corner of the banquet hall. I stood with the thick velvet curtains to my back as I looked around the ballroom.

As expected of the highly celebrated harvest festival, everyone and everything was decked out and practically sparkling. The gold and silver thread and gems embroidered on everyone's clothes shone in the light. When I shifted my gaze upwards, blinded by all the glittering reflections, my eyes fell on the brilliant chandeliers, no less radiant.

This really wasn't my kind of thing. I preferred a back-yard covered in wildflowers to a gaudy ballroom like this. But as I quietly surveyed the hall, I did see a much more familiar face. It was Sia.

For Sia, who had inherited the family business, high society was especially important, and large festivities like today even more so. Sia was surrounded by people and smiling cheerfully as she conversed with them. I had known her since we were children, so I felt quite proud of how mature she was acting. I let my gaze rest on someone near her for a moment but tore my eyes away before she could sense my presence. It was the redheaded young lady, Evelyn.

Was Elvine here? Her gray hair was quite noticeable, so I had expected to spot her in a crowd without any issues. But no matter how many times I looked, I couldn't catch sight of her. It seemed as though she hadn't attended at all, seeing as she was rather reclusive and disliked noisy occasions such as this.

As I mulled over all these things and sipped my drink, I soon realized that I had emptied it. When I twirled my wrist holding the glass once, a waiter quickly came up to me and carried the empty glass away. Instead of getting myself another drink, I stood there and watched the ballroom.

The lime juice had been much sourer than I had expected. The cocktail glass was only half full to begin with, and because I didn't enjoy sour things very much, I had taken my time with it. In other words, the time it took me to empty the glass should have been more than enough for the countess to fix her dress and return to the banquet hall.

The foreboding sense of dread hovering over me did not feel very pleasant. But still, I waited a bit longer. Only when I heard a couple of voices giggling in my direction did I have to admit what was going on.

The countess had no intention of being my chaperone.

She was being truthful when she said she couldn't make my debut a success. Derick and Marie had intended to show everyone that the Severilous family supported me by making it clear that they were sponsoring my debut, and Countess Elcanto was a well-known family friend. With the two of them away from the kingdom, having the countess take care of me was supposed to show that the Severilous family still supported me. But if the countess didn't show up at the ball, with the excuse that there was something wrong with her dress, I would be singled out and labeled as a young noble lady who had absolutely no one supporting her.

Even if Derick and Marie were to come back and try to fix things, first impressions were still very important. It would at least be abundantly clear after tonight that the countess hated me.

Only now did I realize why the countess had come to the ball with me and indicated, in a more abstract manner, that she would not be my chaperone. She was probably worried that I might be able to find a new chaperone even with the restricted time frame. I had expected this. I was more surprised by the fact that she had shown up at all. But she really needn't have worried, because I had no connections to be able to ask anyone else.

I took a deep breath and stepped away from the wall I

had been leaning against. When I calmly turned around, I met the eyes of one of the people who had been giggling at me. I flashed a bright smile while meeting their trembling gaze.

I was definitely at a disadvantage, but I had no intention of backing off now. The countess might have expected me to stand around like a wallflower, unable to do or say anything before slinking home in defeat, but there had been plenty of difficulties in my life that I'd had to overcome on my own.

"Greetings, Lady Albanian."

At my greeting, she gave me a quizzical look. The young lady had light green eyes the color of peridot. Eugenia Albanian. I recalled her full name from the list of nobles I had memorized.

"Who might you be?" she said bluntly.

"Oh my, this must be the first time we've met." I covered my mouth as if in remorse. "I saw you smiling at me and thought we had met before. I am Arwen of the Broschte viscounty."

Eugenia flushed with embarrassment when I commented on her laughing at me. I gave her a pointed look for a moment before drawing my eyebrows together.

"Would you happen to know where my chaperone, Countess Elcanto, might have gone? She told me she was going to the powder room, but I haven't seen her since."

Eugenia's eyes lit up. Her expression quickly returned to its previous haughtiness. "I'm not sure. I heard the countess had left because she wasn't feeling well." She opened her fan with a sharp noise. It was made of bright-colored silk and covered with sparkling gems, making my eyes ache. *I want to snatch that thing away from her.* "It seems like you weren't told. You poor thing."

"Oh my, I see."

She was clearly mocking me again. I took a moment to pretend to be deep in thought before exhaling and muttering quietly, "The duchess and duke will be very sad to hear it."

Eugenia's expression changed. I stopped paying attention to her, only briefly thanking her for the information, and turned away. I could hear her calling me quite desperately, but I didn't spare her another glance.

Step on the weak and stick to the strong. It would have been nice if she had been careful and strong-willed enough to not be so obvious about it. But unfortunately, Eugenia Albanian was not very clever. She wasn't someone I needed to try to befriend. My footsteps were light as I moved away from her and tried to recall all the names I had memorized.

Someone caught my eye right away. She seemed to match her description. When I stepped closer, she turned her gaze toward me, looking neither hostile nor welcoming. I smiled at her.

High society was there for people to make connections. Whether I liked it or not, that was why I was here today.

"It's nice to meet you."

That was why I had to achieve my goals tonight.

CHAPTER
FIFTY-SIX

After a long while, I let out a deep breath and leaned against a wall. The banquet had begun at sundown, but the sky outside had turned completely dark before I was able to escape the crowd.

As expected, people did not exactly welcome me. Half of them considered me to have been abandoned by the Severilous family and feared incurring their wrath by associating with me, while the other half didn't care and weren't afraid of the Severilouses, but saw no benefit in befriending someone with nothing to offer.

None of them were impressed by my greeting them without the introduction of a chaperone, but I still conversed with them as if it didn't bother me, dropping a few bits of information here and there. I intermittently brought up the Severilous dukedom in my conversations. I didn't share anything significant, but I made it sound like I was still close with the family. That was enough to at least assuage those who had been concerned about upsetting the Severilouses by talking to me.

I didn't really like socializing, but I was fairly good at it and wasn't bad at making conversation either, so I was able to achieve my intended goal.

Joanna Eustian, who was closely connected to prominent artists; Valentia Siberius, the wife of the palace's Lord Chamberlain; and Glinda Coolin, who owned a merchant guild that delivered goods to the Schreider territory. Out of the list of individuals I had identified as useful connections to make at the ball today, I was able to have a good conversation with these three and even make plans to meet up again.

Now no one was whispering or laughing while talking about me. Overall, it was not a bad debut. It was enough to turn around public sentiment that had been negative toward me.

I think I did enough.

I walked away from the crowd and headed toward the terrace. Closing the curtains and doors behind me would indicate that I didn't want to be followed. I wanted to be alone.

I felt completely drained. I must have been pretty stressed—because I wasn't even hungry. I hadn't danced at all, yet I felt like I had been run over by a carriage, and my whole body ached.

Maybe refusing all the young noblemen asking for a dance

was just as exhausting. I mulled over this possibility as I walked out onto the terrace and closed the curtains and the glass doors behind me. I let out a long exhale and turned around. Then I froze, unable to draw in my next breath.

Hi," a small voice said.

A silhouette faced me, gray eyes glinting blue with the moonlight. I put my hand over my wildly beating heart and opened my mouth.

"Elvine?"

Elvine hopped off the terrace railing she had been sitting on, and her face came into clear view. It really was her.

"My goodness, what are you doing here?"

Elvine's hair, which must have been put up neatly before, was flowing freely in the wind. Her hair was frizzy to begin with, and tonight it looked like a lion's mane. When I first turned around, I almost fainted from shock. She had been facing away from the moonlight, and with her hair all in disarray, I would have screamed if I hadn't recognized her in time.

I attempted to tame her hair with my fingers and tried to tie it as I scolded her. "If you're going to be out on the terrace, you should have closed the doors or at least the curtains! What if someone came out here and—"

"I left them open so people could come out."

Elvine's simple response left me lost for words, but then I realized that not everyone closed the doors when going out onto the terraces. Those who simply wanted to hold a private conversation would keep the doors open.

Right. Elvine may be quiet, but she might want to talk to new people. When I thought about it, I decided it was mostly my fault for not checking the terrace before entering.

"Sorry. Should I leave?"

"No, it's fine because it's you." Elvine shook her head and sat on the railing again. Watching her swing her legs in a fancy dress had me worried that she would fall off.

"Here. Take my hand." I offered her my hand. She was a sorcerer, so maybe my worries were unfounded, but I was a regular human concerned for my friend. Elvine didn't hesitate to hold my hand. Hers was small and rough.

"So, you were here. I thought you didn't come—because I couldn't find you."

"I was here from the start."

"Then why didn't you go inside?"

"Because I didn't want to mingle with those people." She frowned, and I chuckled at her expression. There were plenty of people who wanted to befriend the only daughter of the Schreider family as well as the kingdom's only sorcerer. It had always made Elvine uncomfortable.

I envied her a little for it. No one would look twice at me if I didn't try my best, and that was what I'd been doing until a moment ago. My smile must have betrayed some of the bitterness I felt, because Elvine reached out her other hand and caressed my cheek.

"Are you lonely, Wen?"

I shook my head. I wasn't lonely. *I just...*

"I just feel like I have nothing."

In the end, the standard for people's appraisal of me was my family name. Their attitudes changed based on which family was backing me—Broschte or Severilous. I was right here, and yet all they weighed were the names. I knew it was inevitable, and I followed suit as well, but somehow it still stung.

"I guess I'm still not used to the Severilous name." The home I loved and the people I loved. But they couldn't be my everything. I valued myself as well and needed more people to see me for who I was. "I feel like none of those people see me for who I am, and it makes me feel like an empty shell. I guess that's making me a little sad."

I loved the Severilous family, but this was another matter entirely. It was a sadness I needed to deal with on my own.

"I see," Elvine said evenly. She wasn't quick to empathize or comfort. Instead, she continued in that same calm voice.

"Wen, you're very charming. Even without the Severilous name, even if you were to be fired from your position at the palace, even if you weren't a noble... you're enough," Elvine said matter-of-factly. "I don't make friends with people who aren't."

I couldn't help but laugh at that added comment. Though Elvine might not have intended to comfort me, it was more than enough to make me feel better.

But she seemed unsatisfied with my smile. I tried to control my expression, thinking she might get mad at me for laughing at something she meant seriously.

"Where is your chaperone?" she said sharply.

I felt like I had been stabbed for a moment, unable to breathe. "She... felt unwell, so she left."

"That's a lie." Her tone was firm. Elvine would sometimes unintentionally rub salt into a wound. "Why did your family leave you with someone like that?"

I couldn't reply.

"If they're close, they must've known what she was like."

"Elvine..." I mumbled, sounding pained. To be honest, it wasn't as though Elvine was saying things I hadn't already thought about. My weak mentality always made mountains out of molehills, and yet I didn't have the strength to deal with the resulting anxiety. If I dwelled on it on my own, there would be no end. That was why I had avoided thinking about it and had intended to talk it out with Marie and Derick once they were back.

"They aren't like that. They all really love me."

"Then why did they leave?"

"It was unavoidable, and you know that."

"There must have been a way. They're the Severilous family. They could have postponed your debut or taken you with them."

When I kept my mouth shut, Elvine stared at me, her usually gentle eyes glinting dangerously.

"Family shouldn't do that. Family isn't supposed to make you feel alone. Even when you're apart, you should have no doubt that they love you. Is that true for you right now, Wen?"

I let out a groan. "I don't know. I know, at least, that it's not their fault."

I truly felt that way. But Elvine blew out a huff of frustration and hopped off the railing. "Wen, can't you live with me? Everyone would welcome you and be your family."

"It's not that simple, Elvine."

Elvine was very keen yet sometimes immature, leading her to occasionally say childish things. I was glad that we seemed to have changed subjects as I tried to comfort her.

But she wasn't done.

"No, Wen. The Schreider family is bound to be better than the Severilous family."

"Only to you, Elvine," I replied playfully, lightly flicking her nose. Of course, Elvine preferred the Schreider family since she'd lived with them for over ten years. But that wasn't the case for me.

Elvine chewed on her lip, apparently still frustrated, before giving me a determined look. "Arwen, you're—"

Just as Elvine was about to say something, someone knocked on the glass door. When I turned my head instinctively, I heard a voice call out to me.

"Wen?"

FIFTY-SEVEN

It was a small voice, like a child whispering. But it sounded oddly familiar.

I didn't even ask who it was and immediately threw open the door only to come face to face with a man. A blond man dressed in ready-made clothes that didn't seem to fit him right. His hair was slicked back with mousse in a ridiculous way, and his face was hidden under a clownish mask.

I could only see his eyes. Those grayish-pink eyes looked back at me.

"Shuell?" I muttered, stunned.

His eyes lit up. Before we could earn any more stares, I quickly pulled Shuell out onto the terrace and closed the door and curtains again.

"Is it really you?"

Even though I asked, I was still confused. There were plenty of young blond nobles, and gray eyes were typically a sign of someone who had altered their eye color with a special kind of eye drop. More importantly, wasn't Shuell supposed to be in Archent?

Even as that thought crossed my mind, I stared at the man as he removed his mask and revealed his face under the moonlight.

"Hi, Wen."

Oh, my goodness.

His features were very, very familiar. It was a face I couldn't help but recognize.

As our eyes met, Shuell gave me a wide smile. "I thought it would take me much longer to find you, but I'm glad it wasn't too difficult."

I knew it was a bold-faced lie. Thanks to his hair being slicked back, his forehead was clearly visible, as were the beads of sweat all across it.

"You... What in the world?" I stammered, unable to form a coherent sentence.

I had no idea what was happening. Why was Shuell, who was supposed to be attending a state funeral in Archent, here right now, looking so ridiculous?

Shuell bowed his head in greeting, having noticed Elvine, while I stood there in utter confusion. "Lady Schreider. I apologize for my appearance."

"No, it's all right." Elvine seemed unhappy with Shuell's presence but didn't reject his formal greeting.

Shuell turned back to me with an uncomfortable smile.

"It's a bit of a long story." He shot a cautious glance over at Elvine. It meant his story wasn't something he could discuss in front of other people.

I also looked over at Elvine. It would have been nice of her to leave, but she had been here first. We couldn't just shoo her away so we could talk.

It seemed as though Shuell had dressed this way in order to hide his identity. I might have already achieved my goal for tonight, but I couldn't bring myself to cross the banquet hall with Shuell when he looked like that.

As I considered our options, Elvine snapped her fingers. Suddenly, Shuell and I began to hover.

"You'll stop when you reach the palace roof."

Shuell smiled at Elvine's curt tone and bowed his head in midair. "Thank you."

"I'm only doing this for Wen's sake."

Elvine's cold voice was the last thing we heard before we rose higher into the air. After a brief moment, we landed on a flat area of the roof next to one of the palace spires.

It was an excellent vantage point for scouting, so I expected it to be guarded. I quickly looked around and found a guard fast asleep nearby, leaning on his spear.

This was fortunate, whether Elvine had used her magic to put him to sleep or if he had fallen asleep on his own. I still intended to chew Shuell out in a hushed tone, but he spoke first, sounding worried.

"Did something happen?"

I hesitated because he sounded as though he already knew everything. Shuell's eyebrows drooped.

"Something did happen."

I couldn't deny it.

"Countess Elcanto had a fight with our parents a long time ago," Shuell said after a moment of silence. "She was never very friendly, but I knew she was a good person. That's why Father asked her to be your chaperone. She wouldn't bully anyone for no reason, so he expected her to do well since she had agreed."

I listened to Shuell's words in silence. They were all true. Countess Elcanto hadn't bullied me without reason, she wasn't friendly either, but she probably was good to everyone else. It was just that, like before, I happened to be at the receiving end of an unfortunate set of circumstances, so distressingly familiar to me now. A set of circumstances for which no one was at fault, but in which there was a clear perpetrator and victim. The kind of situation where I was hurt, but because the perpetrator had their own understandable reasons, I had to bear with it and let it go.

"But I—"

"I thought I shouldn't leave you like that." Shuell gave me a sad smile. "I was sure that the countess wouldn't do anything to you and that you're more than capable of taking care of yourself, Wen. But... I just felt like I needed to come back. I still don't know why. Isn't it strange? I had hoped I would be wrong, though."

I couldn't speak.

"But I guess I was right." Shuell gently wrapped his arms around me. His embrace felt so warm. Only then did I realize that my body had gone cold. "I'm sorry for leaving you all by yourself."

Still the words didn't come.

"It was hard, wasn't it?" His gentle words poured over my frozen heart like liquid lava. I felt strange as I leaned my forehead against his shoulder.

"I'm all right now." The words I hadn't been able to say finally came out. Shuell still looked at me with a worried expression, but I was being honest.

I'm fine now. Now that you've come back for me. Because you managed to find my hidden, inner thoughts. Because you recognized them, even though I always said I was fine. So, everything is fine now.

"So, how did you get here?" Intending to brighten the mood, I smiled.

Shuell seemed to notice and grinned. "I kept thinking that you were probably all right, but something felt off. So, I turned my horse around before we passed the Archent border."

"What?" I was half-joking, but I couldn't help sounding solemn. It took at least a week to reach Archent from Maynard. Did that mean he was out on the road for two whole weeks?

Shuell smiled apologetically at my astounded expression. "I tried to get back as fast as possible, but I was still late."

"That's not important right now." I knew I sounded annoyed, but Shuell kept smiling.

"You're so pretty tonight, Wen." Shuell sounded awestruck, and I looked down at my dress. It was a masterpiece, put together by the sweat and tears of many individuals. The layers of chiffon fluttered at my every movement, and gold thread was embroidered onto it to look like vines, decorated with small diamonds. My curly hair was in a half updo, held up by a diamond-studded hairpin. Overall, it was a very elegant—though not at all simple—beautiful dress, exactly to my taste.

I twirled around for him. The skirts of my dress floated up like rose petals, and the gems on them twinkled in the moonlight. It really was a pretty dress. I hadn't had the time to admire it until now because I had been so nervous. I hadn't even danced yet because the first dance was so important. *What a waste.*

I mulled over it for a moment before reaching my hand out to Shuell. He looked at me, confused, and I smiled.

"Would you take my first dance, my lord?"

"What?" Shuell blushed brightly. He'd planned on being my dance partner to begin with, so I didn't know why he was being so bashful now. He seemed flustered, his eyes slowly returning to their normal color and darting back and forth.

"But my outfit, Wen..."

"It doesn't matter. Mine is pretty. And yours does suit you quite well."

You could see the lines left by the comb in his hair, and there was an unusual lace detail on his dress suit. I giggled, and Shuell rolled his eyes before giving me a very formal response.

"As you wish, Lady Arwen."

We clasped our hands together—as we had done many times before—and began to dance without any music. Shuell's eyebrows drew together, and I laughed. I had placed my feet on top of his. Shuell sighed but didn't shake me off him. We danced together slowly, step by step.

"I feel like I'm not worthy of taking your first dance."

"Not worthy? If the son of the Severilous family isn't, then who is?" I gave him a playful smile, but hearing my own words made me remember something, and I came to a halt.

Come to think of it, I never envied you. Isn't that strange?

He had everything, and I had nothing. If he were in the same situation as I had been today, he would have held his head up high because he was born a Severilous. Even then, I hadn't thought about those differences between us all evening.

I was lost in thought for a moment. *Have I never envied you?*

I slowly followed his lead. When we twirled around with the moon behind our backs, I suddenly remembered something from our childhood.

Oh, right.

I *did* envy him back then.

It was when we were very young.

CHAPTER
FIFTY-EIGHT

My smile must have looked a little sharp because Shuell, with a worried gaze, came to a halt after a slow turn.

My memory of feeling envious of him was so embarrassing that I wanted to forget about it. And I felt bad for Shuell as soon as I recalled it. I would've liked to keep it to myself, but I lightly stepped away from him. Shuell mirrored my movement.

After a moment of silence, I said, "Did you know I once envied you?"

Shuell, still looking at me uncertainly, opened his eyes wide and shook his head. "You envied me, Wen?" He seemed genuinely surprised, which made me laugh.

"Yes, I did."

To Shuell, this might have been surprising because when we were young, I had always been quicker at learning things than he was. But that wasn't what I was talking about.

"You have a loving family." Even as I said it, I recognized that I was being vague. The reason I envied him wasn't so pitiful and sad. Shuell didn't respond and simply listened to what I had to say, which helped me to continue. "It was something I could never have, and I was jealous of you for taking it for granted. I would get angry whenever you fought with your parents. Because I would have been so happy just to have parents, and yet you seemed dissatisfied."

I thought back to how pathetic and childish I had been. Back then, Shuell had been just as kind as he was now, but sometimes I'd hated the way he acted because he was immature. And sometimes, it would make me think very dark thoughts.

What if I hadn't saved you? for example. *Then you would have lost your loving family, which would have made you the same as me. And then I wouldn't have to envy you or have such a hard time.*

I hated myself for having thoughts like that, and I hated Shuell for saying that he liked me even though he knew nothing. That was how it was back then.

"But at some point, those thoughts stopped occurring to me. Do you know why?" My soft mutters flowed into the summer breeze. I felt relaxed. "Because you were so beautiful. I just couldn't hate you."

I vaguely remembered one summer afternoon. A young Shuell, smiling brightly under the sunlight. His smile had reminded me of a budding rose, small but real. I had been standing in the shade, and the sight of him had brought tears to my eyes.

Shuell had always had a beautiful smile. Unaffected by the hardships of life, so innocent and beautiful. It was a smile that I had protected.

If I hadn't saved him, what would have happened to him? He might have been able to smile like that someday, but it would have taken many days of crying and suffering. Because I was aware of that, Shuell's pure joy was blindingly beautiful to me, and my heart was full at the thought of having protected it.

After I saved him, I thought that if all my hardships and suffering were to protect his smile... it was all worth it.

"So, I couldn't dislike you anymore." I had no intention of ever telling him that I had once regretted saving him, and I wondered whether that made it difficult for Shuell to understand what I was saying. But still, I wanted to tell him as much.

"That's good, then," he answered, his voice light. "The present is what matters. Whatever happened in the past, it's fine as long as you are all right now."

"You're right."

Our responses were lighthearted. We stepped away from each other. We acted as though we had just finished dancing in a proper ballroom and acknowledged each other formally.

I chuckled to myself at our antics, but Shuell was acting oddly. He was biting his lip as he looked at me, his eyebrows drawn down. I raised one of mine, because I knew that was the face he made when he was disappointed or had done something wrong.

"Do you really not dislike me now?" he blurted out before I could question him. He seemed a bit embarrassed by the wording and paused, but he then raised his large hands and gently took mine. "Please don't hate me, Wen. I'll do better, all right?"

The pink eyes staring down at me were wide and filled with unshed tears. He looked so much like a puppy begging for food that I burst out laughing.

"And how exactly are you going to do better?"

"I'll do anything." His reply was quick, but he seemed unsure of what else to offer, and he looked crestfallen again. I couldn't help myself and pulled one hand from his grip to ruffle his hair. *What a cutie.*

"You're already doing really well. And if I did still dislike you, I wouldn't have told you all of this."

"Really?" His eyes began to sparkle again, showing his relief. Shuell took my hand, which he was still holding, and raised it to his cheek. "Wen, please tell me if you start to dislike me..." he mumbled, his voice trailing off weakly.

"I think you'd cry if I did, though."

"No, I wouldn't," he replied, pouting. He raised his head, wide eyed. "Is that why you're not telling me? Because I might cry? I promise I won't. Won't you tell me?"

He looked at me with puppy-dog eyes once more. I laughed, seeing that I had nothing to confess to him.

"I'll tell you if that happens. I promise." I held out my pinky like we did when we were kids. "What will you do if I tell you, though?"

"I'll change. Until you stop disliking me."

His answer made me feel strange. Shuell had always been like this. He really was devoted.

"What if it's my fault and I'm just taking it out on you?"

"You would never do something like that." His gaze was firm as he said this. His trust seemed absolute.

"Why do you like me?" I asked suddenly. It was something I had asked before, whether to him or to myself. The question had occurred to me several times. "I think you see me as some amazing, wonderful person, but..."

Sometimes, it even felt like he worshiped me, like I was some sort of deity. I couldn't bear to say that out loud, though.

"There are plenty of better people out there." *People who*

aren't as sensitive. People who are more beautiful and brighter. Just like you. "I'm much more insignificant than you think."

It was such an obvious fact that it didn't even make me sad. Shuell seemed to disagree, judging by his frown.

"There are many much more wonderful people than me," I continued. "You're old enough to have realized that by now."

Unlike in our childhood, when he hadn't had much contact with others, Shuell had since entered high society. He would have met all kinds of people and raised his standards accordingly. It was only natural that he would have met countless people who were better than me.

"Why do you love me?" I didn't feel pathetic or sad in any way. I was just curious.

Shuell's face had softened. "Just because."

"Just because?"

It was a short, almost shameless answer. As I narrowed my eyes, Shuell simply looked at me with a clear gaze.

"Why do you like me then, Wen?"

"Hmm?"

"You like me, don't you?"

I was left bewildered by his sudden, straightforward question. Did I like him? Of course, I did, but...

You make it sound... different.

Better words needed to be invented for these types of situations. There should be separate words for liking someone as a friend and liking someone as a romantic interest. I nodded as these thoughts went through my head.

"Do you have a reason?" he asked.

A reason? I took a moment to think before I answered. "You're kind, and sometimes quite cute, and..."

What else?

I had intended to start rattling off all the qualities I liked about Shuell but came up short. As I stood there, at a loss for words, Shuell laughed.

"Those are just qualities about me. Does that mean you wouldn't like me if I wasn't kind or cute?"

"I guess I still would," I mumbled quietly. It was like I was admitting defeat.

"It's the same for me," Shuell said almost melodically. He kept his voice quiet, as if taking care not to wake the sleeping guard. "Sure, there may be plenty of better people out there. But that doesn't matter. It's not like I started liking you so I could gain something, Wen."

I didn't know how to respond.

"All I see is you." Shuell smiled shyly. "Was that too cliché?" He let go of my hand and took a step back. I stared at him as he avoided my gaze. Even under the pale moonlight,

I could see how red his cheeks had gotten. "You tend to see me as a little kid, so... I want to act more maturely. But maybe I'm just not good at acting cool and smooth."

I stared wordlessly at him, as if I was mesmerized by the moonlight.

"What do you mean, I'm the only one you see?" I finally managed to say, my voice trembling. "What in the world..."

I wasn't sad or happy. No, maybe I was both. I wasn't quite sure myself. My raw emotions spilled out, too heavy to keep inside.

"What does that even mean?"

I had never been told by anyone that I was their everything. I smiled with teary eyes, feeling both happy and sad.

CHAPTER
FIFTY-NINE

I had never slept so deeply as that night after I returned to the mansion.

I had no reason to show up at the other festivities since I had participated in the first night of the harvest festival, the countess had returned to Elcanto manor, and Shuell was back. My whole body was finally able to unravel after being so on edge, so my wonderful night of sleep was probably very predictable.

There were two to three more weeks until Derick and Marie would return. I had nothing to do before then, so it was like I was suddenly on vacation. I took my time in the morning, getting up only once the sun was high in the sky and leisurely sauntering out of my room. None of the household staff had anything to say about my disorderly state. They actually looked very cheerful.

I pulled one of the maids aside to ask what was going on. "Did something good happen?"

Her answer was instant. "Of course! Our young master has returned." She seemed genuinely pleased, her face alight with joy. "He may not be able to set foot outside of the house—outside of his room, even—because he is so unwell, but still, he has returned! We have to celebrate!"

Her enthusiastic waterfall of words felt like a sudden cold shower.

"What?"

"Did you not hear, my lady?" The maid tilted her head to one side in confusion. I nodded as I put my hand on my forehead.

Of course. As healthy as he may have been, there was no way someone would be fine after riding a horse nonstop for a week.

"Where is Shuell now?"

"He's in his office."

"He is not in bed?" My voice was displeased, and the chatty maid grew wary. I gave her a pat on the head before walking away.

Shuell's office wasn't too far away. When I knocked on the door, I heard him say "Come in" from inside.

"Wen?"

"Shuell..."

Shuell seemed to have been looking over some paperwork, dressed casually in a shirt, before he looked up. On seeing that it was me, his eyes crinkled into a smile.

"Wen, your hair is a mess."

Do you really feel like teasing me right now? I stomped over to him and pinched his nose with my fingers. Shuell let out a whine of pain as he pretended that it hurt.

"Come on, Wen. Look at this, it's—"

"I don't care. You need to get changed and get into bed right now. Why are you working when you're sick?"

Shuell looked up at me with a puzzled expression. "Sick?"

"I heard everything. Stop trying to hide it. One of the maids told me all about how sick you are."

"But I'm not." With a look of someone wrongfully accused, Shuell got up and put his forehead up to my face. "Here, touch it. I don't have a fever, and I'm certainly not..." He had started off strong but trailed off. "Oh, right. That."

"Would you mind telling me what exactly is going on?" I crossed my arms over my chest and took a step back from Shuell. I hadn't been able to detect any heat from him when he stuck his forehead in my face. His cheeks were slightly flushed, but it looked more like a healthy glow than the feverish disposition of a sickly patient.

He doesn't look sick. So why was that maid so cheerfully talking about the news that her master was ill?

"It was my excuse to miss the state funeral in Archent.

I told them I wasn't feeling well and that it was most likely an infectious disease. Since they were closing the borders, I wouldn't be able to have any medicine delivered from Maynard, and it would be bad if I infected others."

I listened quietly, feeling my expression change into a frown. "Is it all right for you to do that?"

Shuell grinned, as if he wasn't worried at all. "As long as I don't get caught."

"No, I mean—how is that even possible? People must've seen you at the ball last night, and you said you got here on horseback. Were you wearing a mask the whole time?"

"No one recognized me at the ball, and I only got on horseback once I was a long way from the royal messenger. I was in a carriage before that," Shuell explained nonchalantly, shrugging. "Anyway, that's why I'm currently recovering. At least that's what the general public thinks."

"You really are unbelievable."

Is this the recklessness of youth? Groaning, I put my hand to my head. Unlike me, who always went with the safest route, sometimes frustratingly so, Shuell tended to have an adventurous side. He was just like Rietta...

"Did Rietta not want to come with you?"

Shuell simply smiled. I kept my mouth shut because I could tell by that smile that he had suffered enough. It wasn't as though he really was sick, and this wasn't going to get him into trouble, so that was that. Just as I let myself feel relieved, Shuell looked at me with a glint in his eyes.

"Wen, there's something I want to tell you."

"Hmm?"

"You said you wanted Broschte to become a vassal of the Severilous dukedom. It's been taken care of," Shuell said, sounding gleeful, and the news made me brighten up.

"That quickly? I thought the elders might have their complaints…"

"It's not as though they have anything to lose from it, and they've known about you staying here for years, so they didn't seem very surprised."

"Still, that was quick. I figured it might take a while."

Shuell gave me a pleased smile when I sounded impressed. I had noticed that he had been busily taking care of something before they left. It must have been this.

"So, what do you want to do now, Wen?" Shuell asked me. His eyes sparkled, as if he was eager to do anything I asked of him.

Calm down, pup.

I chuckled before taking a moment to think. There wasn't anything in particular I wanted to do. Research really wasn't my thing to begin with.

"I just want to rest."

"Hmm?"

"I've never had such a long vacation. I just want to be lazy and rest."

While I was at the Academy, I had always been busy studying, even during vacations, to catch up on the learning material. There was no reason for me to be such a diligent student, as I was forced to be in my past life, so I felt a bit of remorse for all that time I had wasted. But now, I have the chance to rest, so I decided to do so to my heart's content.

And there's a reason I'm calling it a vacation.

There were a few things I was still unsure about, but I needed to discuss them with Derick and Marie. It wasn't something I could take care of on my own. I didn't have anything else to do, so I might as well idle away.

I smiled happily at the thought.

My vacation was over in the blink of an eye. I did nothing but eat and sleep. I felt more like a lazy animal than a human, but every time I felt a bit guilty, I merely yawned and rolled over.

I ate everything I wanted to and slept whenever I felt like it. When I got bored, I would visit Shuell in his office and watch him work hard. Then I would nap on the couch there.

I spent most of the two-week vacation asleep. I must have been exhausted—because I was always sleepy. I felt I would have to do something big once Derick and Marie were back, and this break was in preparation for that. Shuell sometimes shot me envious looks but never stopped me from lazing around, and my precious vacation time passed as I wiled the time away.

Good times always flew by quickly, so it felt like the date of Derick and Marie's return arrived in a flash.

"Wen!" Rietta came flying at me like a bullet and jumped into my arms. It was such a tight embrace that it felt more like an attack than a hug. I let out a cough. *Ah, there goes my precious vacation. Farewell.*

"Welcome back, Rietta."

"I missed you!"

"There, there." I stroked Rietta's hair before handing her off to Shuell and turning to Marie. I smiled warmly as I welcomed her, and she stroked my hair.

"You did well, Wen."

"Thank you."

After Marie, only Derick was left to greet. He looked a bit gaunt and seemed to have lost some weight, but he didn't seem to be in a terrible mood. He beamed at me.

"We're back!" Derick wrapped me in a tight embrace. He

was as gentle and cheerful as always. "How have you been? Were you scared without us? Have you been sleeping well? You seem like you've lost some weight."

I shook my head. If anything, I must have gained weight from doing nothing but eating and sleeping for days on end. I shot Derick a worried look. I had something to tell him, but I was still apprehensive about bringing it up.

"How was your debut?"

Yes. That.

Fortunately, it hadn't been terrible, but everyone knew by now that Countess Elcanto despised me. Derick had left me in the hands of a good friend. If he found out that she had mistreated me, he would feel terrible. But rumors had already spread, and it was impossible for Derick not to find out even if I didn't tell him about it myself.

I had confided in Shuell countless times, wondering whether it was a good idea to tell Derick, but we concluded that it was the right thing to do. We knew that it would be better for him to hear it from me than from someone else.

I took a deep breath. "Derick, Marie, there's something I need to tell you."

CHAPTER
SIXTY

It didn't take long to tell them. There wasn't much to explain anyway.

As soon as I was done, I studied their faces cautiously. They had listened to me calmly, but I couldn't tell what they were thinking based on their expressions.

Uh-oh.

As soon as my gaze met Marie's, I changed my mind. Her expression was similar to her usual impassiveness, so I didn't notice it immediately, but she had a terrifying look in her eyes.

"What would you like us to do?"

"No, I'm not asking you to do anything..."

I was trying to dissuade Marie, whose response was immediate, from taking action, when I felt a slightly trembling but warm hand take mine.

"I'm sorry, my dear." Derick's brown eyes seemed darker than usual. His shoulders looked slumped, as if they were weighed down by guilt and sadness. "I didn't intend for this to happen. We had a bit of an argument with her when we first took you in, but that was so long ago that I thought she had changed her mind. We had no idea she would mistreat you when we asked her to take care of you. Still, I should have looked into it more carefully. I don't know what to say, Wen."

"I'm all right," I said sincerely. I really was all right now. I had only brought it up so that it wouldn't be as hard for him to hear. But Derick and Marie's expressions were still somber.

"I intend to make a complaint to the Elcanto family."

"Marie."

"We cannot let this slide. Not only did she disrespect you, but she also slighted us by doing so." Marie's tone was firm even though I tried to hold her back. I looked over at Derick pleadingly, but he shook his head, also unwilling to let this matter go.

I had no intention of making a public complaint. The rumor that the countess had caused, saying that the Severilous family had ousted me, would die down quickly. I also didn't want Derick and Marie to have to part ways with their good friend.

And most of all, I had no intention of letting this go either, although I had a different method in mind.

"Please don't make a public complaint," I asked them

firmly. They gave me stern looks, but I smiled. "Could you request a visit to the Elcanto manor instead?"

Henrietta Elcanto looked troubled as she pressed the tips of her fingers against her brows. This happened quite frequently at the Elcanto household, so the members of staff were holding their breaths.

It had been a month since this heavy atmosphere had taken over the house. To be exact, a month had passed since Henrietta, who had always been so even-tempered, had started to look furious and a little guilty.

When Henrietta had been asked by the duchess and duke to be Arwen Broschte's chaperone one month ago, she was exasperated. She couldn't understand why the Severilous family would put up with the harm to their name by keeping Arwen close. They had taken in and raised a child who had no value whatsoever, and all she had achieved was to become some lowly secretary in the palace. Henrietta, who had voiced her concerns back when they had decided to sponsor the girl, was outraged to hear that they had decided to continue to support her after helping her make her debut in high society.

She intended to refuse on the spot. She was ready to forcefully dissuade Kendrick from being that girl's chaperone, so taking on that role herself was out of the question. But in the middle of writing her reply, refusing their request, Henrietta changed her mind.

The Severilous family would have no trouble finding another chaperone, though not one as good as her. And any noblewoman who accepted the request of chaperoning Arwen, whose reputation left something to be desired, would surely be so intimidated by the Severilous name that she would do her best to help the girl with her debut.

After a moment of mulling over the matter, Henrietta had written her reply. She had agreed.

The duke and duchess had left for Archent, and Henrietta had been left at the Severilous estate with Arwen. She had never met Arwen before, but the girl turned out to be an elegant young lady. If it hadn't been for her circumstances and status, the title of noblewoman would have suited her much better than it did Rietta. Henrietta had consciously made an effort not to feel any regret about this. Ifs and maybes had no meaning. And she couldn't do the job poorly, either.

She decided to take on the role of the villain. She was harsh to the household staff and had something to complain about in every one of Arwen's mannerisms. She did this in order to get Arwen to give up, so as not to have to chaperone her. But Arwen was much more patient than Henrietta had expected. Her etiquette was already impeccable, but she made sure that even the tips of her fingers were perfectly in place, as if to challenge Henrietta's critiques.

Henrietta was well aware that what she was doing was underhanded, but she couldn't just stand by and watch her friend go down the wrong path. So, she tormented Arwen. She was harsh to the girl when she asked, with her doe-like eyes, why the countess hated her. That was the first time Henrietta managed to shake Arwen.

Arwen, who had never said a word about being starved and tormented from morning till night, looked at her with clear pain in her eyes, and for the first time, she confronted Henrietta. After Arwen left the reception room that day, Henrietta was conflicted. She didn't feel like touching her tea anymore. It would have been easier if the girl was selfish, interested only in the Severilous fortune. Though Arwen's uprightness made it hard to dislike her, whenever Henrietta remembered the girl's lowly station, she couldn't bring herself to be nice to her.

Despite her conflicted feelings, Henrietta tried her best to achieve her goal. But she failed. Arwen still managed to make a successful debut even without a chaperone. Henrietta's attempts at preventing this, even against her own conscience, had been futile.

And today, four days after Duke and Duchess Severilous had returned from Archent, they'd sent a message, stating their intent to visit the Elcanto manor. Henrietta puffed on her cigarette, thinking about how she would be seeing her friend again. The reason for Kendrick and Marias' visit was obvious. They were going to complain about her clear dismissal of their request.

"My lady, a guest from the Severilous estate has arrived."

"Tell them to come in," Henrietta replied as she got up to greet her old friends.

But when Henrietta looked up, her face froze. The person in front of her was not who she had expected.

"Hello, my lady. It has been a while." Arwen bowed her head to Henrietta, wearing a gentle smile. Her demeanor was unwavering, just as before.

Henrietta was quick to react, having spent so many years in high society. She eyed the girl coldly as she sat back down. "I expected Marie or Derick, not you."

"I apologize for not making it clear earlier. I thought you might refuse my visit, so I asked the duchess to send the request herself," Arwen said blithely. Henrietta didn't respond, and Arwen gave her a look that was hard to read.

"I know you still hate me," Arwen said after a moment

of silence. It was the second time she had raised this subject, but unlike the first, her voice wasn't trembling.

"I do," Henrietta lied. She assumed that Arwen resented her regardless of why Henrietta had to treat her that way. She had no intention of skirting past that resentment by making excuses, saying that she had her own reasons and that she bore no ill will against her. She held her head high, elegantly, even as she expected an onslaught of criticism.

But the words that followed were completely unexpected. "I understand. I also know why you had no choice but to hate me. Regardless, you were also aware of the fact that I wasn't to blame."

Arwen spoke quietly. Her attitude was that of one calmly reprimanding a younger sibling rather than blurting out her hurt feelings. It bothered Henrietta, but she had to admit that she was right.

"You were wrong. You made a mistake." And then, Arwen quietly but firmly declared, "We will not be able to become friends. You hated me, and I remember that too well." As she spoke, Arwen looked upright. There was no trace of hesitance or insecurity in the way she held herself. "One day, you will most definitely regret having missed the opportunity to make a wonderful friend."

Once she was done, Arwen let out a long breath and

smiled brightly. She looked satisfied, as though she had laid down a heavy burden. "That is what I came to tell you."

Behind her smile, Henrietta could see the faces of her old friends. As she stared at the girl in a daze, Arwen said goodbye and left the room.

It felt as though the strange anxiety that had followed Henrietta around for the past two weeks had suddenly grabbed her by the neck. She let out a huff of laughter.

"One day, you will most definitely regret having missed the opportunity to make a wonderful friend."

Arwen's words continued to echo in the room even though she was already gone.

To be continued...